A Monaco Minute

Book 2 in the Monaco Series

Kaya Quinsey Holt

coco rose books

A Monaco Minute
A Coco Rose Books Publication

Copyright © Kaya Quinsey Holt

All rights reserved.

First paperback edition 2023

978-1-7771022-6-5

For my boys—Ryan and Leo.

All is fair in love and racing.

A Monaco Minute

PROLOGUE
Nicholas

Ten years ago

N icholas breathed in the languid Monaco air on a warm July afternoon. His mother passed him a croissant, still warm from the oven, as the three of them sat on their balcony. His dad was already dressed, wearing a shirt with Nicholas' racing number on it: 62.

Nicholas had already given an interview to the press earlier that week about why he had chosen that number.

"I chose the first number, six, because that's the number of people in my family: me, my mom, my dad, my late adoptive parents, Isabelle and Roland Stefano, and my grandmother, Marguerite Levant. I chose the second number, two, because I've had a second chance to build my family and my life."

The interviewer, Violet Macintyre, had smiled. "What a beautiful answer. Thanks, Nicholas. We're looking forward to seeing how you race today. If it's anything like what we've seen earlier this season, I think we're in for a treat."

Nicholas had smiled politely and thanked the interviewer, as he came to be trained to do by the media team, before leaving to go off to the side. That entire week turned out to be packed with interviews, media and press appearances, and parties. It was exhilarating, exhausting, and the best time of his life. His mom and dad had watched every single one of his races from the sidelines with eager smiles the whole way.

His dad passed him a cup of espresso, putting on his sunglasses to shield himself from the bright morning light. "We couldn't be more proud of you, Nicholas," Freddie said to him for what felt like the millionth time. "You've not only gotten one of the twenty seats in Formula One, which is such an accomplishment in itself, but you're fighting for first place this season so far. I mean, everyone expected you to do well, but I don't think anyone expected *this*."

His mom shook her head in disbelief. "I mean, you've been working so hard for the last few years. Well, since you got started racing. And your driving shows it. We always knew you could make it to Formula One and be one of the best drivers on the grid, but you've done it so *early*!"

Nicholas smiled shyly. "Thanks mom and dad," he muttered, feeling his cheeks becoming pink. Even after all of his success, he still never felt totally comfortable receiving so much praise. He supposed he had better get used to it.

"You've worked so hard," his dad continued. "I don't think you've taken much more than a few days off of practicing in a row since you were what? Nine?"

"Nine, that's right," his mother added, nodding her head.

It was true. A lot had changed in his life. One of the most notable, other than reuniting with his biological parents, was his steep ascent into the racing world after getting a seat on the Formula 4, later Formula 3, then Formula 2 team, before that incredible day when his dream was realized: he was officially had one of the coveted twenty seats on the Formula One track. His trajectory appeared similar to his dad's; of course, he was doing it all a little sooner than everyone had expected. Today would be his fifth race as an official F1 driver. There were twenty-three races total. He had either won or come in a close second for each race so far, which was unheard of for a rookie.

He sent a silent prayer to the sky, thanking his Ma and Father, who he often thought of and fondly remembered. From somewhere deep within, he felt they were helping guide him and perhaps throwing a little luck his way.

"I'm a little nervous," he admitted. "Racing in my hometown. So many people are counting on me." Although he had developed a reputation for being fearless on the track, he could only admit such things to his parents.

His dad smiled at him and clapped him on the shoulder. "You'd be crazy not to be, son."

His mom looked down at her left hand and smiled. "And just think. Your very first Monaco race happening on our anniversary. My, how the time flies."

Nicholas could remember the day his parents got married with crystal clarity. It was a warm summer day, not dissimilar to this one. He was nine-years-old and chuffed to have been asked to be the best man. They had gotten married in a park overlooking the sea and his mom had worn a white dress with off-the-shoulder straps. Mostly, he remembered that at the reception, they had a chocolate fountain that he was given unlimited access to. It was funny the things that stuck in his memory. His crush at the time, Miranda, had come to the wedding accompanied by her dads. Who knew that crush would have turned into such a complicated, wonderful relationship?

"I've got to give Miranda a call," Nicholas said, looking down at his phone. Over the years, that girl had become his very best friend. She had been there at his first race. He had seen her through heartbreak as she navigated her on-again off-again relationship with Markus, who was back then and continued to remain a thorn in his side. He turned out to be too focused on racing to think about having a girlfriend. Well, perhaps he had thought about it a little more than he cared to admit. Although fear wasn't something that most people thought about when it came to Nicholas Stefano, there was one thing he felt absolutely terrified of. And he had never gotten the courage to tell Miranda how he felt.

He left the balcony, leaving his parents to talk amongst themselves, and went to his bedroom, carefully shutting the door. Even though he was sixteen, sometimes he still felt like that nine-year old who had just stepped into that apartment for the first time, hands nearly shaking. He held his phone in his hands, putting it on speakerphone, waiting to get through. He expected that she would be getting ready for race day. Perhaps she had a moment or two to spare.

"Hello?" came Miranda's giggling voice. There was someone in the background talking to her.

"Hey," he said, feeling his heart flutter in his chest. "How's it going?" For some reason, lately he had felt especially self-conscious whenever he talked on the phone with her.

"Stop it," she muttered in a whisper to whoever was in the background. Nicholas' heart sunk. "Okay, sorry, hi!" she said direction into the receiver. "Are you ready for your race?"

"I hope so," he said with a laugh. "Are you with someone?"

"Oh, just Markus," she said, a hint of awkwardness to her voice. "He, uh, surprised me."

"Right," he managed. "Well—"

"—Have you done your routine?" Miranda asked, interrupting him. His heart softened. Typical Miranda.

Nicholas laughed. "Not yet. But I will." Miranda was the one person, other than his parents and the team principal, who knew about his pre-race routine: gargle with mouthwash three times, take twenty deep breaths, and visualize the grid twice, winning once, and passing no one since he is at the front of the pack.

"Well, I'll be thinking of you," she said. "Break a leg. And keep your wits about you. This isn't going to be an easy race."

Nicholas felt heat rising in his body. The two of them spoke the same language. They breathed the same passion. He could hear it in her voice, in her tone. He was exactly the same way.

"I can't wait," he said, meaning every word.

In the background, he could hear Markus saying something to Miranda in what sounded like a frustrated tone.

"I should go," Miranda said, a little too brightly. "But seriously, Nicholas. Good luck. And I'll be thinking about you. Whatever happens today."

Nicholas didn't want to jinx anything, but he was pretty sure he could feel it too. A tingling sensation all throughout his body. Like something amazing was just around the corner.

"It's bound to be interesting. I'll catch up with you after the race, okay?" he said, hoping Markus could hear him. "I'll take you out for dinner at that new seaside restaurant you like. What's it called again?"

Nicholas knew exactly the name of that restaurant. He had already made reservations, but he wanted to play it cool.

"Le Bernadin? Oh, Nicholas. That would be great. Okay, I've really got to go, but I'll be thinking of you."

Nicholas smiled. "Okay. Bye Miranda."

"Not bye," she said playfully. "See you later!"

He laughed. "Right. See you later."

He hung up, thinking that Miranda was one of those people who thought about the danger involved in car racing frequently. She reminded him more about the dangers of racing more than even he thought about it, and he was certainly not naive to the risks involved in the sport he loved. Earlier in the season, she had burst into tears when she saw him at the end of one of his races after he had a near crash with another driver.

Nicholas headed back to be with his parents. He needed to shift gears. He couldn't think about Miranda or the gnawing sensation inside of him that Markus was back in her life… *again*. Not that he was the jealous type. But it didn't help that he had secretly been in love with her since he had met her.

But he couldn't think about that. Today was race day. He had to get his game face on. Over the years, he had become an expert at compartmentalizing his life. When he needed to shift to racing, he had laser focus and nothing could distract him from the race.

"Everything all right?" his mom asked, a note of concern in her voice.

Nicholas forced a bright smile. "Great. She's doing well."

"I meant with you, silly," his mom said with a laugh. "How are *you* feeling?"

Nicholas laughed. "I'm ready."

"I have no doubt," his dad said. "I mean, look at the kid? He's a natural. Plus, his mom is the most passionate driver out there. You've got genetics on your side," his dad teased. All of them knew that his mom hated driving but adored watching races.

"How is Gene? Is he recovered from his injury?"

Gene Stromball was his biggest rival and a three-time world champion driver. Nicholas had hit the ground running when he got started, and had been Gene's only real competitor since his domination of the sport for the last three years. Today he had one main objective: to beat Gene. And Gene wanted to win more than anything. Luckily, so did Nicholas.

"Apparently his left thumb is fine," Nicholas said, citing what he had heard amongst his team. "The lesson seems to be: you shouldn't ride a horse during racing season if you've never tried it before."

"Well, use everything to your advantage," his dad said seriously. "Formula One demands that of you."

Nicholas nodded and checked his watch. "Right. Well, I should get going. I'll see you after the race, mom?"

His mother smiled. "For sure. I'll be there with mémé. She'll be waving to you, Nicholas. Make sure you send a wave in her direction!"

"I always do," he said with a smile. "Dad, you ready?"

To make an already ideal career even better, his dad was his manager. It certainly helped having a dad with a Formula One career like his had. Besides, Freddie had told him that retirement just wasn't his cup of tea. He needed something else to focus on. It turned out that he was an even better manager than he was a racer, and that was certainly saying a lot.

"Ready. Let's go, champ."

Racing had a way of captivating every ounce of his attention. His heart pounded in his chest. He had placed second in his qualifying lap, meaning that he started in second place on the grid. Gene was ahead of him.

One person popped up in his mind. Miranda. He certainly hoped that she was watching. To him, that mattered almost as much as winning, which said a lot. Trying to shake thoughts of Miranda from his mind, he heard a voice come through his earpiece.

"Go win, kid," came his dad's voice.

Nicholas took a steadying breath. "Will do, dad."

He looked to the stands, where he knew his mom and grandmother were watching. Although they couldn't see him, he sent a nod in their direction and a silent prayer to his late adoptive parents.

This was it. Nicholas knew that he had already won in the lottery of life. Sure, there had been challenges, difficulties, and unconventional attributes about his upbringing. But knowing where it had all led him, he would never have it any other way. The lights began to blink, signaling that the race was about to start. Nicholas felt the familiar joy, excitement, exhilaration bubbling up in him and he pulled down his helmet.

3-2-1. The race was off.

"Woo hoo hoo hoo" he shouted to no one in particular, pressing his foot all the way down on the gas. One thing not everyone knew about racing Formula One cars: it was incredibly, seriously fun.

Nicholas navigated the twists and turns of the grid with precision. He listened to the voice in his ear. His speed, timing, and navigation of the grid was impeccable. Breaking at all the right points, accelerating when he needed to. The car was performing just as he needed it to.

"This is it. This is my time!" Nicholas cried out, with the finish line in sight as he managed his final lap. Gene was just behind him. He was in first place. This was almost it. The win was so close, he could nearly taste it.

As Nicholas flew through the finish line, cheers erupted from the fans.

He had won the Monaco Grand Prix. He had won the race! Nicholas screamed in relief and delight. His team ran to the track, waving and putting up one finger, signaling his podium finishing place. They were hugging and shouting at one another. It looked like a parade.

Tears welled in Nicholas' eyes as he pulled to a stop.

"This is it, son. You did it! You've won!" came his dad's voice through his earpiece.

Nicholas was shaking as he stood up, emerging from the car and raising his hands above his head. His team and the crowd roared their applause. It was the best feeling in the world.

"Thank you," Nicholas yelled to his team. "I couldn't have done it without all of you. This win is yours!" he said, pumping his fist in the air. His whole team shouted, hooting and hollering, and his dad came into view giving him the thumbs up, a giant smile plastered on his tanned face.

As his team embraced him and he shook millions of hands, adrenaline pumping through his veins, he looked up at the crowd and waved to his grandmother. He was sure she was watching with a keen eye, just as she always did.

A few girls came up to him, presumably family members of the team, asking for his autograph and pictures. Of course, he was obliged and delighted.

"You're my favorite racer," one of the girls said, clinging to the signed piece of paper like her life depended on it.

Nicholas smiled and gave them a wink before turning to meet his dad, the team principal, and head to the podium where he would stand in first place. He couldn't wait. He was Nicholas Stefano. And he planned on this being the first Monaco Grand Prix he would win of *many* races he intended to come in first. He flashed a grin while trying to memorize every second of that moment. After all, he was just getting started.

Buckle up.

ONE
Miranda

Now

S ometimes, it only took a single turn to throw off the entire circuit, turning the perfect lap into one of the worst.

"What a circus," Miranda commented, watching as a sports team made their way through the Nice airport towards the departure gate, dodging people snapping pictures with their phones. Golden sunlight poured through the large glass terminal, displaying the French Riviera's sun and clear blue sky. Although it was February and cool by the their standards, it was much warmer than where she came from.

The French woman at the airport café, who spoke English with a whisper of an accent, passed Miranda her cappuccino. "You'd never believe who went through here earlier today. Are you into car racing?"

Miranda shook her head. "I haven't kept up in the last few years."

The woman continued. "Well, it was some hotshot young driver. He had his whole entourage with him. Two men almost got into a fistfight trying to get his autograph. Imagine!"

"Absolute madness," Miranda agreed.

"All the sports stars make their way through this airport. But I only recognize the racers, especially Formula One. You watch Formula One?"

Miranda paused for a moment before she shook her head. She hadn't let herself think about racing in a long time.

"It's practically a religion here."

Miranda checked her watch. "I don't want to be late. It was nice talking to you."

She made her way to the outdoor platform where taxis were lined up to pick up passengers, spilling her cappuccino slightly and leaving a mark on her brand-new cream sweater.

While holding her cappuccino with her right hand, she realized she should have had her phone. It was that moment when what should have been the perfect start came to a halt.

She wasn't the type to write things down. Or print them out. She lived off of the information she saved on her phone. Her Uber app? Useless without a device to use it. Where was the address her dad had given her? It was somewhere in Monaco, and she knew only that much.

Reaching into her worn leather purse, she carefully checked that she hadn't lost the photograph she carried with her in the fold of her Moleskine journal. At least that was still there. A picture from ten years earlier—the old-fashioned kind—of her sixteen-year-old self and her two dads, smiling on a beach along the Riviera. Back when they all lived in Monaco. Back when people still got photos developed. Back when there were still three of them.

"Lost, you say?" asked the lost and found attendant, who didn't seem concerned despite Miranda's near tears.

"It's gone. I've checked everywhere I stopped after I got off my flight. The restroom, the café..."

Her suitcases rested at her feet, carrying the necessities for a year. Her arms had grown tired, lugging the two enormous bags behind her through the airport.

"Ah, *désolée*," the attendant said with a shrug, although it seemed as if he couldn't be less concerned to Miranda. "There is a line for the taxis there." He pointed towards an ever-growing line that waited on the pavement outside the glass doors. "Where are you going?"

"Monaco." She once would have gotten a thrill from saying that word. She would have been over the moon a year earlier to see where she was today. Now, she took a deep breath and tried to inject some enthusiasm into her tone. "Okay. Well, please call me...actually, you can't call me... I'll check in tomorrow to see if my phone turns up. Okay?"

The man barely nodded before returning to what he was doing on his computer. Miranda could practically feel fumes coming out of her ears.

"*Bon voyage!*" she heard the man call from behind her.

She waved in acknowledgment before trudging towards the taxi line. But she wasn't here for a vacation. This certainly hadn't been the homecoming she had anticipated.

As she waited in line for a taxi, she took a deep breath of salty air and smoothed the ceases on her linen pants. Seven hours and forty minutes seated for her flight had them looking rumpled. They felt too tight, but they had looked so good on the model on the website. Her dad, Chris, had always worn linen. Somehow, his never seemed to wrinkle.

Miranda's turn for a taxi had finally come. She trudged towards the glossy black door with aching arms and heavy luggage. She felt immediately relieved at the thought of sitting down somewhere air-conditioned and quiet, even if she would soon be arriving in Monaco with the task of figuring everything out once she got there. She could call someone. *Do payphones even exist anymore?* She could almost hear her dad's voice telling her she should have written things down.

After the people ahead of her were gone, and she was the only person waiting, a taxi finally pulled up, and it was her turn. She opened up the door when a man's voice came from behind.

"Excuse me, I need this taxi."

She stopped and turned around. She couldn't make out much of the man's face with his oversized sunglasses, scarf, ball cap, and high-collared jacket, but she couldn't help noticing his smile. He had immaculate, straight, white teeth. She tended to notice these things after having braces twice during adolescence. He smiled at her, surely to appease her for his ridiculous request. She knew guys like this— good-looking guys who were used to getting their way.

The taxi driver was already stepping out and grabbing Miranda's luggage to put into the popped trunk. The man took a step towards the taxi. He had expensive-looking luggage and an air of confidence. This was going to be his unlucky day.

"Sorry," she pulled a face. "I'm practically on my way."

This was the man's cue to patiently wait for another taxi. She turned to open the door and took a seat, sinking into the plush seat, when she turned back to take a better look at this person. He acknowledged her with a slightly flustered expression and nodded before returning to his phone.

Her eyes zeroed in. His *phone.*

Then again, what was the harm in helping someone out? Especially when they had the one thing that she needed.

She requested the taxi driver wait for just a moment before she got out again, approaching the man.

"Where are you going?" she asked.

He looked up from his phone with surprise. "Monaco."

It figured. From what Miranda could barely make out of his face behind his sunglasses and ball cap, she noticed that he had exceptionally high cheekbones. There was something familiar about him. Attractive and confident, standing straight as an arrow and moving with a sense of refinement. He seemed European, but she couldn't detect an accent. Probably a celebrity of some sort? He was already putting his phone in his pocket and looking at her expectantly.

Some type of celebrity, Miranda figured. Not famous enough to recognize immediately but vaguely familiar in an unassuming setting.

"So am I in?" he asked, making her think he already knew the answer.

If Miranda faced the facts, the truth was that without her phone, she didn't know the address in Monaco she was going to. Although it was technically where she had been born and lived for most of her life, she wouldn't be able to navigate it with the help of a GPS. She put her hand on her hip, examining him from top to bottom for potential red flags.

"Are you a murderer?" she asked flippantly. She was only half-kidding.

His expression turned to one of amusement. "The most psychotic of the sort."

"Are you a criminal?"

"Undoubtedly."

Miranda peered at him, desperately tuning into her senses to see if she detected any warning signs from this stranger. So far, no glaring alarms were going off. Besides, there was the taxi driver as a witness if things got weird.

"If you were either of those things, you would probably try to convince me that you weren't. All right, we can share the taxi. But I need a favor from you, too."

***

Using the man's phone, she texted her dad, Kyle, who was back at their home in Montreal, Canada, telling him that she was all right and had lost her cell. Thank goodness her dad had the same phone number since she was sixteen and it was one of two numbers she remembered by heart, seared indelibly into her memory. It still didn't feel real to think she wouldn't need to remember her other dad Chris' phone number.

She could barely wrap her mind around being back in the Riviera. They had left ten years ago. In that first year after they left, she had felt so much homesickness that she had gotten back together with her ex, Markus, and done a whole long-distance for a few months. She even saw a few of her old friend's races that year. They left Monaco after her dad, Chris, got an excited career opportunity at a gallery in Montreal, and they agreed it would be an adventure. She had been sixteen and experienced a medley of emotions related to the move—heartbreak to go, excitement to start something new, and a plan to return as soon as soon as she turned eighteen.

That first year was harder than she had expected. She clung to an image of herself in Monaco that she later realized she had outgrown, including getting back with her ex.

It had taken some time, but eventually she found her footing. She focused on where she wanted to go rather than where she had been. She put her head down, and finished high school with soaring grades. The five years she had spent at medical school in Ireland were a blur. She had returned to Canada to do three years of residency in family medicine before pursuing additional qualifications in sports medicine. Then, she had found her job at the sports medicine clinic where she had worked for a year—the same year that her family situation had taken a turn.

Needless to say, her plans to return to Monaco full-time always got pushed.

When her and her dads left Monaco, a family trip to return was planned. But skiing holidays, exploring Canada, and school trips had gotten in the way. Her dads had even spoken about returning to Monaco in their retirement. It was tentative, but the possibility was always there.

Never in a million years would she have anticipated returning under the present circumstances.

"On second thought," Miranda began, breaking the silence that had spanned their entire taxi ride so far. "If you were a murderer or criminal, maybe saying you weren't would be too easy. Of course, you would say that you were to be disarming."

The man continued to look out the window and laughed lightly at her comment. "I'm not a murderer. Or a criminal, for that matter."

She chuckled, expecting him to further the conversation. After all, she'd been the one to break the ice. But her laugh faded and the two of them were left again silence. The only sound was the clamber of traffic from outside the taxi driver's slightly ajar window and the Bossa Nova music that played quietly over the speaker system.

Who does this guy think he is? Miranda carefully assessed the man beside her from the corner of her eye. He had yet to take off his sunglasses and hat in the car. But she was used to eccentric types from Monaco.

Miranda looked down at his phone in her hands, which she had used to log into her email and pull all the necessary information she needed, like the address of the rental company where she was picking up her keys, her new rental apartment in an adjacent town, and necessary phone numbers. It was all written down in her journal. Miranda leaned against the window, taking in all the Belle Époque buildings with their swirly iron balconies, palm trees in straight lines, and the terra cotta walkway adjacent to the sea and grey stone beach along the Promenade des Anglais. A lot remained the same from her memory. And a lot had changed since she'd last been there too.

Chris, her dad, had died of a heart attack earlier that year. It was sudden. And if she was being honest with herself, it still didn't feel real. If she woke up realizing that the last year had been a dream, she wouldn't have felt surprised.

But it wasn't a dream. She knew that. Chris had been in excellent health his whole life. In fact, he had just completed his very first marathon the year before. She had even helped him train for it. When he collapsed at work, emergency responders had done what they could to save him. He had been brought to the hospital, but they later told her that it was too late.

Seriously—she was a doctor. Had she missed signs that this was leading up? In her head, she had mentally replayed every interaction with him, asking herself if she had missed something. She was left without any answers. It was a shock then. It *still* was a shock now.

And it had been even more shocking when she and her other dad, Kyle, learned of Chris' wishes. Neither of them had known the contents of his will prior to his death. They certainly hadn't expected what it said.

To their surprise, Chris hadn't sold all their property when they left, like they had previously believed. In his will, he had written about an underground parking spot which he still owned, where his beloved vintage car was still parked. And it was right here in Monaco.

He had left it to her.

She had to go see it. When she had been booking her ticket, Kyle had offered to travel with Miranda to retrieve the car with her. But her dad had struggled in his own way over the last year. She figured it would be painful for Kyle to come back without his husband of many decades, especially to the place where they had built their early life together. She may have come months earlier if it hadn't been for her recent developments on the job front. And the relationship front, for that matter.

The man beside her cleared his throat. He sure didn't seem much in the mood to talk. Nor had he introduced himself. Still, she had met stranger people in her travels.

That's just fine, she thought. *I'm not really in the mood to talk, either.*

She looked out the window, viewing the glimmering Mediterranean Sea to her right and the opulent, timeworn buildings to her left along the Promenade through Old Nice. Tourists posed for photos on the sidewalks and locals sped past them on their motorbikes. She had a soft spot for the city. She had her first drink in a bar there. As a teenager, she laid out on those pebbly beaches for hours. She'd shopped, dined, and explored the narrow streets of *Vieux* Nice until the sun had set and got home hours after the moon had risen.

She logged out of her email and double-checked that she had written down all the necessary information. Mission accomplished. She delicately poked the man on the shoulder to give the phone back to him.

"Thanks," he replied simply, taking the phone and turning back to look out the window. He had the better view, seated to Miranda's right, and appeared to be making the most of it.

She couldn't blame him. The view was spectacular. Yachts glimmered along the coastline. As the bustling Promenade faded into the distance, they snaked along roads that Miranda was certain were one way but nope—another car would miraculously squeeze past them with blinding speed from the opposite direction.

"I always get so nervous along these winding roads," she found herself saying aloud. She had learned to drive on streets like this and her heart had raced even back then.

"They're not so bad once you're used to them," he replied.

"You drive them often?" she inquired.

"Hmm," he murmured, looking out the window.

Miranda looked out her own window and fiddled with her watch. She knew she should just let things be between them. He clearly didn't want to talk. But she felt uneasy. When she felt that way, she just couldn't help herself from talking.

"So," she pressed. "If you're not a murderer or criminal, what do you do?" Perhaps they knew some of the same people. Not that she knew many people from Monaco anymore—it had been ten years since she left. But Monaco was a small country and an even smaller community.

The man kept his gaze firmly out the window. "Oh, this and that."

Miranda rolled her eyes. A big ego was the absolute worst character trait, according to her. She figured that the least he could do was make some diminutive chitchat. And then they could be on their way. After all, she had gotten him a taxi to Monaco, just as he had seemed to need. She shifted in her seat. They zoomed along a road with stonewalls and mountains that peaked out of the hills in the distance. This was starting to look very familiar.

She could practically hear her dad, Chris, saying his usual catchphrase: "Kill them with kindness." He had encountered a lot of big egos and personalities working in the art world. The worst that could happen was that the man beside her remained stony.

"Isn't the view stunning?" Miranda asked brightly.

"It is."

She drummed her fingers on her knee, crossing then uncrossing her legs. They felt cramped after hours on the plane. "So why did you need this taxi so urgently?"

Finally, he turned towards her and she felt a frisson of delight that she'd hooked him. Already, the awkward silence was beginning to melt away. Wasn't that the way it always went? Sometimes, people just needed an icebreaker, she figured—just like at the beginning of those uncomfortable virtual meetings that her clinic had hosted at the beginning of the pandemic. The awkwardness always thawed by the end.

"Why did you need my phone?" he responded in an unreadable tone.

"I lost mine at the airport," Miranda explained. "Total nightmare, as you can imagine."

The man pulled a face. "That is the worst."

"It's not exactly the best start," she disclosed. "I'll be in Monaco for a year, and this isn't exactly how I imagined it."

Her words hung in the air, and she wondered if he'd just leave them there.

"That's a long time to spend in Monaco," he eventually stated.

"It is," she agreed.

After a moment, he looked at her. "What brings you to Monaco?"

"I'm starting a new job," she said, glad that he was finally talking. What she said was true, but only partly true. She hardly felt like disclosing the real reason she had begun looking into returning to Monaco. The job had been unexpected. Her circumstances had been unexpected. A lot in the last year had been that way. She felt butterflies in her stomach just thinking about it. She waited eagerly for the man to ask more about it. It definitely didn't feel right to add the *other* reason she was here—what had brought her back in the first place.

From out the window, she zeroed in on a pair of dads walking along the sidewalk with their daughter in tow, and she felt a pull at her heartstrings.

After a beat, the man nodded. "Well done." He turned back to look out the window.

"Thanks," Miranda managed. She turned to look out the window and rested her head on her hand. She might as well join him.

How humiliating. Miranda hardly wanted to be the person who forced people into conversations. She hated those people. Back in Montreal, on the metro, if someone had tried to strike up a conversation with her, she would steadfastly keep her gaze ahead of her, fixating on something random like an advertisement, and smile politely. Or look down at her phone. She was *never* the instigator. Those people were the worst. Now, she was doing that to this man who wanted to keep to himself.

Suddenly, she felt a pang of guilt for never having chatted with those people on the metro before. Had they just wanted some sort of connection, too? She pushed it aside and focused on the drive. The last year had made her a different person. More chatty, more anxious, less present.

Outside her window, the buildings gradually became more opulent. The grey and green mountains towered in the backdrop against the cerulean sky, blanketing the densely packed country facing the sea. Luxurious-looking cars decorated the narrow roads and pastel-colored buildings with fancy columns brought her back to a simpler time in her life.

They had arrived.

The driver expertly wove by parks with flawless grass and geometric flower arrangements. She felt they were close to her destination, and the car slowed to stop as they approached a large, luxurious-looking cream-colored building covered in moldings and more of those exquisite iron balconies.

"Would you like me to get closer?" the driver asked. "It might be awhile with all this commotion."

Outside the grand entrance was a bevy of people holding cameras, clearly waiting for someone to exit. Was there someone famous who lived there? Miranda craned her neck to look out the window for any sign of someone she recognized, feeling her hopes rise. It could be any celebrity.

"Is this your stop?" she asked.

"Yes," he replied.

But he didn't move. In fact, he turned and looked at Miranda. A warm feeling spread within her. He was objectively attractive, she noted. Even with his hat, sunglasses, and scarf pulled high. And there was something extra familiar about him. Her brain was working hard to place him.

"On second thought, we can drop her off first," he told the taxi driver.

Something began to click in her memory. That voice. She had heard it before.

The blinkers clicked as the taxi slowly turned around, and the man visibly relaxed into the seat.

"I would appreciate it if you didn't mention this to anyone."

Miranda nodded but felt the tension rising. She took a closer look at him. He *looked* like someone she had seen before. Who was he? And why the secrecy? Should she be worried? She didn't even know his name, she realized. This was basic safety 101 that she had thrown out the window. For what? An adventure? A good story? And she had hardly experienced either of those in this car ride.

"No problem," she said. "I mean, I don't know anything about you, so that isn't hard." She laughed a bit uneasily.

The man looked like he was working something out in his head and had just come to a final decision. . She felt a frisson of surprise as he took off his sunglasses and hat for the first time since meeting her, revealing molten eyes with dark, thick lashes. Suddenly, she could see his face.

"I'm Nicholas," he said.

Like a light switch being flicked on, it dawned on her. Her stomach clenched as her breath caught in her throat. The man's eyes burned into hers as if looking for something. She *knew* him. Not just from today. A sudden flashback from him as a boy, staring at her with those same eyes. The same dark lashes. The way his eyes creased at the corners. His dimples and the slightly uneven up curve at the corners of his mouth.

She hadn't thought about him for years. But back when she had been in Monaco, he had been all her sixteen-year-old heart could focus on. Her heartbeat thudded in her chest with each memory that surfaced of the two of them, and her breaths came in short bursts. Nicholas seemed to notice as his eyes dropped to her mouth. Now, he was all grown up.

"Nicky?" she breathed. "Nicky? Is that you?"

TWO

Nicholas

Ten years earlier

C ars were piling up behind them, honking noisily on the one-lane road.

"Come on," Miranda called from the front seat. "Can't you go any faster?"

Nicholas' lungs were on fire. "I'm trying as best I can!"

The old car had conked out. Worse, he'd pushed it to its limits. Turns out trying to show off his speed didn't work on just any car. Leave it to him for this to happen to Miranda's dad's beloved vintage beauty.

He would have dropped dead of embarrassment. But then the car pileup behind them would be even worse.

Diesel fumes and thirst didn't pair well, especially in the scorching Mediterranean summers pushing a stalled car. He heaved as he gave the old vehicle another shove from behind. The sun hung low in the sky, creating soft-focus golden light for all the tourists who visited Monaco this time each year. A stone wall to his right had pink flowers streaming off of it. He wanted to point out the flowers to Miranda, but it wasn't the right time. He had walked this route home a million times before but had yet to notice how narrow the roads were. Or long.

"Steer to the left!" he hollered as the car veered towards the ones parked to their right.

"I am!"

She was back in the driver's seat, steering to the garage, or at least somewhere they could park it without causing a significant traffic jam. Why wasn't there any parking?

They finally found an empty space and narrowly squeezed into it. The delayed cars zoomed past them with varying degrees of frustration. Miranda hardly looked in a good mood herself. He couldn't blame her.

"For this to happen today, of all the days." Miranda stepped out of the car and assessed the vehicle for damage. Not that there was much to see.

Nicholas figured he had done something to the engine based on the noises it was making. He lifted up the hood and propped it open. Everything about this machine was meticulous. Vintage. A few thousand kilometers on it.

Broken.

He pushed the thought of Miranda's dads out of his mind. Christian would understand—although it was Chris' car, Miranda's dad had always had a more relaxed attitude to them getting into mischief. Kyle would more likely be the one who would be upset. A small part of him still felt like he had to impress Kyle but he had long ago won over Chris. He'd known Miranda's family since grade school. Ever since he met her as children, the two of them had been inseparable. It was typical of Miranda to convince Chris to let them take the car out for a spin on Nicholas' birthday.

Now sixteen, the day wasn't turning out how he had envisioned. The two of them were starting the twenty-minute drive from Monaco to Menton, a nearby small coastal town. He loved the colorful houses, the nooks and crannies, and the incredible beach of the small city between France and Italy. But more importantly, Miranda loved it. She was always trying to see more of the world. If he didn't have to, he might never leave Monaco. The two of them were based there and still lived with their parents. On weekday evenings after school, like this one, they liked to explore the neighboring towns along the Riviera.

They would look at the map and choose a city. Better yet, sometimes they would just drive and find somewhere new.

But today wasn't about being spontaneous. Today was more than that.

Nicholas shut the hood with a thud. He really didn't know what was wrong with it.

"Just think," Miranda said, leaning against the car with her arms crossed. "In a few years, we'll have our own cars."

He forced a smile. He was standing on the sidewalk, hands in his pockets, the sky above them turning the perfect hue of strawberry pink. "Don't you think you're going to miss it here?"

He wasn't sure if he meant Monaco in general or that specific moment—being stuck with him and her dad's busted vintage car on his birthday and all the potential moments like it that could have been.

She crossed and uncrossed her arms.

How heartbroken he'd been learning that Miranda and her dads, Kyle and Chris, were moving to Canada. They were leaving in a week. It still didn't feel possible to him. He was sure he'd come across as sullen since the news was broken. "It's not like you to be so quiet," she had told him. He had so much he wanted to say. But every time he opened his mouth, the words never came. But it wasn't like Miranda was opening up a bunch, either. She had barely mentioned Montreal to him since they first discussed it.

"Honestly, I don't know what to feel," she said.

Honestly, he felt annoyed by the comment. Wasn't Miranda going to miss him? Didn't they have—something? He was sure it wasn't just him imagining things.

"What on Earth could be better than this?" he asked, gesturing wildly towards the shocking pink bougainvillea, the clear sky, the ornate buildings, the tepid air around them. Not to mention the Mediterranean Sea, which was always a short walk away.

Miranda shook her head slowly and gave him a sad smile. She stepped towards him, and his heart dropped into his stomach. Her eyes were fixed on his, and a few hair strands had fallen from her ponytail.

She was the picture of the perfect summer to him. The perfect life. Her phone buzzed from the pocket of her shorts, and her attention snapped from him to the text. She wrinkled her nose.

"Markus wants to know if he can tag along," she said, reading from the message.

Nicholas let out a sigh. "I know he still likes you, Miranda. Just because you broke up with him doesn't mean there aren't still feelings on his side."

She put her phone back in her pocket. "I'll answer Markus later." Her attention returned to him, and suddenly, he felt self-conscious. "In answer to your question—yes. I'll miss it here."

Nicholas nodded, but her words were like a balm. He needed to know she'd miss Monaco. He needed to know she'd miss...*him*.

The car began to make a gurgling noise, giving him a jolt. They both turned towards the vehicle. It stopped. He looked at Miranda, cautiously walked to the driver's seat, and put the key in the ignition. The car revved to life like nothing had ever happened in the first place.

Miranda grinned and hopped into the passenger seat. "Let's go, Nicky," she said.

She was the only person who could call him Nicky. He hated the nickname. But he loved the way it sounded coming out of her mouth.

He put the car into gear and felt the familiar stir of being in the driver's seat with an adventure ahead of them. "Let's go."

Seven more days until she left.

They walked towards the clear blue water. The sea was still except for a couple of lazy ripples that seemed to come from deep beneath. The mountains to their left gave a glimpse of Italy in the distance. As they walked along the soft sand, palms swayed to their right. The colorful town was humming behind them with foot traffic from a blend of tourists, locals like them, and families packing up after a day at the beach. Menton was one of his favorite places along the Riviera. It was colorful, with old buildings in bright pink and yellow shades. He loved getting equally colorful gelato and walking along the seaside promenade on evenings like this one.

Tonight, he'd chosen mango, and Miranda chose pistachio, both in cups.

It was a gorgeous town. But most deliciously—no one knew him there. It sometimes gave him some relief, especially considering his famous racecar driver for a father and his bourgeoning racing career. An Italian-speaking family greeted one another with head nods and *buona seras*.

It was June, and the beach was already crowded. It would become practically gridlocked come July and August. It felt strange to think there might not be many more evenings ahead where his presence would go unnoticed. He'd only ever been recognized as the son of Freddie Ridgeport in Monaco, where racing aficionados flocked from every corner of the world. Soon, he would be the one who was noticed. Life was about to change in a lot of ways.

Couldn't Miranda just stay?

The salty smell of the sea mingled with the sweet gelato. The sand squished between his toes. Even though he wore sandals, he had grainy bits grating against his skin.

"Are you having a nice birthday?" Miranda asked, stealing from his gelato with her spoon.

One word: *Yes.*

"So, can I expect another signature Miranda gift for future birthday?" he asked, brushing his hair out of his eyes. He wore a plain watch that he fiddled with.

"Oh, you don't think I'll get you anything after I leave?" Miranda replied with mock hurt. "In all the years you've known me."

Nicholas' mouth twitched. "All the most ridiculous gifts I have gotten, I've gotten from you. The flying lessons?"

Miranda pulled a face. "The guy said he was a licensed pilot."

"The scuba lessons?"

"Also, an honest mistake. The guy said he had a boat. How was I supposed to know we'd take a fishing vessel?"

"And that it would attract sharks..."

"We left with all of our fingers and toes," she laughed.

"And don't forget that he asked if we could gut the fish after our near brush with death," he couldn't resist adding. The corners of his mouth rose, reminiscing.

"You'd make a great fisherman if racing doesn't turn out how you hope it does," she said, putting her empty gelato bowl onto his and taking a few steps ahead of him along the beach so that she could feel the waves against her bare feet.

Miranda didn't know about his contract. He hadn't told her. No one knew except for his parents. He had never kept a secret from Miranda before. He had a hard time understanding himself at times. Why hadn't he told her?

"I've got something to tell you," he began, catching up to her on the sand.

"The car was part of my gift to you," she said, clearly not having heard him. "I know how much you love old cars. Or 'vintage' as you say. Not to keep, of course."

Nicholas smiled. "It was a great gift." They lapsed into silence and kept walking; the only sound between them was the waves. He took a few deep breaths before mustering the confidence to finally say it. "I've been offered a spot on the team. I'm—I'm going to take it."

Miranda stopped and turned to him. "Seriously?"

Nicholas nodded. He could feel his cheeks turning furiously pink. He had confided to her that a Formula One team had been interested. But he hadn't told her *how* interested.

"The news is breaking tomorrow," he told her. "I signed the papers earlier this week."

Miranda threw her arms around him, making his heart skip a beat. "Nicky! This is incredible news." She pulled away from him. "How come you didn't tell me?"

He shrugged. "I guess I just wanted a few more moments of normalcy. A lot is about to change."

She looked suddenly nervous, but it was only for a moment.

Her radiant smile made him feel as excited as he had when he first got the news. "You're going to be amazing," she said confidently.

"I'm going to be spending a lot of time traveling," he said. "I'm going to miss it here."

Miranda looked around, her eyes unexpectedly glassy. "I'm going to miss it here too."

He wanted to ask her to stay. He wished she would. He hoped that some things could stay the same. A drop of gelato that had melted over the edge dripped onto his hand.

"Promise we'll keep in touch?" he asked, inwardly wincing at how he sounded.

But Miranda replied with a steady sureness. "You're my best friend. We'll always be. I promise."

Just like passing that checkered flag first, her words hit him right in the heart.

THREE
Miranda

Now

A glimmer of something resembling panic flashed over Nicky's face as she spoke. Clearly, he didn't recognize her either.

"Nicholas Stefano?" she repeated, just in case she'd gotten it wrong.

"That's me," he replied in a tone she didn't recognize.

Was he...nervous? She stared at him, and he stared back, his expression blank. Indeed, he would be excited to see her once he realized.

"I'm Miranda," she said slowly. "Miranda Thatcher?"

As if in slow motion, recognition appeared to dawn on him. First, his eyes—the moment she said her name, they began searching her face. The muscles in his jaw loosened. His brow relaxed. Slowly, the corners of his lips curled into a grin.

"No way!" He looked at her as if for the first time before his face burst into a smile. He laughed, and it made her laugh, too. "Miranda? Miranda. My God. It's been a while. How—why—" He smiled between laughter, shaking his head as if he, too, couldn't believe it. She could barely believe it herself.

Instantly, she was transported. She had gained Nicholas' trust in elementary school as his friend, and they had been inseparable. As they got older, she had jumped off cliffs into the Mediterranean with him. She had raced go-karts with him. She had learned how to drive in his car. Days had been spent at hidden beaches along the coast. Night had been spent exploring the Riviera's hidden nooks and crannies.

She hadn't thought about Nicholas Stefano in years. Strange to think there had been a time when he had been all she could think about.

"What a small world," she finally said, still smiling. "Not entirely surprising to find you in Monaco, but to find myself in a taxi with you..."

"Definitely not what I thought today had in store," he said, his ear-to-ear grin still plastered on his face.

"Me neither," she said, matching his exuberant tone. "Gosh, what has it been? Nine, ten years?"

Nicholas scrunched his brow as if trying to remember—the same way Miranda remembered him doing when he was a kid. "About that, probably," he said.

All of her worry subsided as memories of her childhood surfaced. What a way to return home—by running into her old friend. He had been more than just a friend if she was being honest. He had been her very first crush. Later, her first love.

He had never known that, though.

When her family moved away, her sixteen-year-old self had been heartbroken. Getting over him had taken longer than she cared to admit. Of course, he had never known how she felt about him, and she certainly wasn't about to share that with him now.

If only her younger self could see them now. She wished she'd applied some lip gloss.

"What have you been up to these last few years?" she asked, genuinely curious. The tension between them was thawing, and she felt more at ease.

"Driving, mostly," Nicholas spoke in a slightly guarded way.

Light a light bulb, and memories of Nicholas racing came back full throttle. She'd left Monaco when his career was about to take off. His career had been lightning-hot in the first few years he was signed. She had gone to see his races when she could in that first year that she had moved. But they had drifted apart. His career was on a rocket. She was in a different country. And then she'd double down on her own career path.

She recalled reading years ago about how his career had "crashed and burned" and he was ruthlessly cut from his team after being in the sport for seven years. She wondered what he'd been up to since then.

"How is your dad, Freddie? And your mom, Charlotte?"

"They're good. They spend a lot of time traveling these days."

"And your grandmother?"

His face warmed. "Still as lively as ever."

"How about your dads—" Nicholas began, but Miranda cut him off before he could finish.

"—And are you still driving at all?" she asked, immediately regretting it. She could be such a klutz when she was nervous.

"Oh, here and there."

She pulled a face. Nicholas had always wanted to be a world champion. He had desperately wanted to be the best driver of all time—the same way his dad had been. She had followed Nicky in the sport for the first few years after she moved, and he had won a few podiums, including the Monaco Grand Prix in his first year of racing. But never a world championship.

"Well, I'm sure it's not an easy sport," she said with resolve.

Nicholas looked unsure of how to reply. "Thanks."

She crossed and uncrossed her legs, thinking about what to ask him next. The thing she wanted to talk about least, even more than his stalled racing career, was her dad.

"Look, I didn't mean to be standoffish earlier," he said quickly.

Surprised, she laughed. "I had almost forgotten about that."

"I don't usually dress like this," he said with a slight chuckle, gesturing to his hat.

"Oh?"

"It's just that things in my life are... complicated," he said carefully. He rubbed at the crease between his brows, his jaw becoming rigid again.

Miranda nodded slowly. "That's all right—"

"—So you don't mind keeping this taxi ride between us?" Nicholas asked, giving her a strange swooping feeling in her stomach.

"Sure," she replied. "No problem."

"Thanks," Nicholas replied with visible relief. "Now that that's settled, why don't we stop by a little restaurant I know quite well. Are you hungry?"

After the last year, Miranda considered herself relatively immune to shock. But today, she was stunned. The restaurant Nicholas took her to wasn't open to patrons yet, and the chairs hung off the marble tables. Old-fashioned and well-preserved was how Miranda would have described it to her friends outside of Monaco. It was the kind of place that her late father would have loved. She felt a twinge at the thought of him, like she always did these days, and pushed it out of her mind. Besides the one person wiping down the bar, it was just the two of them. The restaurant still needed to turn on the music over the sound system.

"So, how is it we never kept in touch?" Nicholas asked as they walked in.

Miranda shrugged. "I'm probably one of the only people who doesn't use social media. Well, I did," she corrected herself. "But I deleted it really fast. It's too addicting."

"How do you stay in contact with people then?" He looked genuinely stunned.

"Texting, mostly. But I left before Instagram and all that became popular, so I didn't keep in touch with anyone. Remember the first year I left when I was coming to your races? We emailed for a while." She hadn't thought of those emails for years and laughed at the memory— she had been obsessed with finding the proper wording.

"That's right! So you didn't keep in touch with anyone else?"

"No one regularly. I actually got back in touch with Markus, if you remember him..." she trailed off.

Nicholas' brow creased for a moment. "It's hard keeping in touch. Maybe you'll reconnect with more people. Who knows?"

"That's true. I hadn't exactly planned on running into you."

As they took a seat, Nicholas mentioned that he was a friend of the restaurant's owner—they had apparently known one another for years. Unsurprisingly, he had an expansive network here, which wasn't hard to believe considering he had never lived elsewhere. To him, Monaco was "home and always would be." Miranda had spent the last ten years living in Montreal and traveling to other corners of the world. But being back in her original home base felt like a breath of fresh air.

"So you're in Monaco for the full year?" Nicholas munched on a buttery, flaky breadstick that the waiter offered them.

Miranda twirled her fork between her thumb and index finger. "Yeah. I got an exciting job," she said with a grin.

"Oh yeah? What kind of work do you do?"

"I'm a sports medicine physician," she replied, putting down her fork. "I focused my research on sports performance. There's a sports rehabilitation facility in Monaco looking to take on someone to help treat high-performance athletes. Anyways, I've signed a contract for one year," she said. It certainly wasn't a lie. It just wasn't the whole truth.

The truth was that she was in Monaco for her dad. Plain and simple. But people didn't want to hear that. And frankly, she didn't want to talk about it. Or think about it, for that matter. She did anything to *not* focus on her dad's death. In a moment of self-reflection, she had briefly allowed herself to entertain that she got the job to distract herself from the real reason she was in Monaco. Still, she didn't see the point in dwelling. It was painful and uncomfortable, and there was no solution. It was done. He was gone. She even avoided the subject with her other dad when he tried to talk to her about it. Wasn't coming back to Monaco enough?

Nicholas' eyes widened. "Wow. Sports medicine. That's interesting. What sport do you specialize in?"

"Oh, all of them," Miranda replied. "The clinic I'll be at is legendary. I'll be working under the supervision of Doctor Elbar. Athletes from all over the world come to work with him."

"And, it seems, practitioners do, too."

Miranda nodded. "It wasn't planned, though. An old friend reached out to me recently after, uh, some stuff came up," she began, skirting around how Markus reached out to her after reading about Chris' death from one of Kyle's social media posts. "We caught up about each other's lives. He helps run the clinic."

"Don't tell me—Markus?" Nicholas asked, his tone unreadable.

She nodded. Her relationship with her ex was on good terms. Markus had always been kind and he had been a comfort when she moved away that first year. But they were never meant to be. After that long-distance portion of their relationship nearly ten years ago, they had mutually agreed it wasn't going to work. It seemed that Markus knew that too. She hadn't gotten the impression that he was looking to rekindle their old flame.

"We caught up," Miranda explained. "I told him I was interested in working somewhere new. He mentioned that a clinic he manages was looking for a physician. I looked it up, then looked into it further, and before I knew it..."

"Here you are."

"Exactly. I've been working in the field for about year," she explained.

"How'd you end up doing sports stuff?"

"Sports medicine," Miranda corrected him. "I had planned to be a family doctor. Pediatrics had even crossed my mind. But one day, someone talked to me about wanting to change their life. He wanted to prove to himself that he could run a marathon. He was a runner but didn't believe he could manage the distance. Running was his outlet. It had gotten them through difficult times—putting one foot before the other. I gave him some tips, talked with him about it...it just kind of sparked something in me."

She didn't mention that her dad, Chris, had been that runner. She couldn't help but smile thinking of the day that he had confided in her and asked for her off-the-record professional advice. He had been one of the healthiest people she knew. When she was a little girl, Chris had run up and down the seemingly endless staircases in Monaco on weekend mornings as the sun rose before the tourists took over.

Seriously, how was he not here anymore?

Nicholas smiled. How hadn't she recognized him upon first seeing him? His sunglasses and hat were neatly placed on the table. In that weird getup, she guessed that it made sense that he had been unrecognizable. After all, that was his goal.

"And how about you?" Miranda asked, feeling herself leaning forward inadvertently. She pulled back. This wasn't the time. And she was in no state to think of anything like that. "I've barely learned a thing about you. Except that you're still into racing?"

From behind her, she heard the waiter snort from laughter. Nicholas shot him a look.

Nicholas' mouth twitched as if deciding on something. He opened his mouth as if to say something before closing it. "Yes. But, I'm lately I've been spending more time focusing on my life outside racing lately," he said finally.

Miranda nodded. "And what does your life outside of racing look like?"

Nicholas took a swig of his sparkling water. For a moment, his face opened up. She hadn't realized how guarded he had been until his wall dropped.

"Can you keep a secret?" he asked, his face suddenly serious.

Her interest was piqued, and she leaned forward. "You're not going to tell me anything weird, are you? Please tell me you are," she teased. It felt good to let her guard down, too. It felt good to laugh. For months, she'd had nothing but people offering their condolences, treating her like she'd break into tears at any moment. This was refreshing.

Nicholas appeared to enjoy the banter, and his face broke into a smile. "That depends. No, but in all seriousness, I've been trying to make some changes."

"Okay, so what kind of changes?"

Whatever openness Nicholas had momentarily felt vanished as quickly as a racecar sped along straightaways. "You know what? Never mind. It's not that interesting." He was clearly changing the subject. "Tell me more about the kinds of clients you'll be seeing."

Miranda had a croissant, freshly squeezed orange juice, and a café crème. This was turning out to be a phenomenal breakfast. She bit into the last remaining piece of buttery, flaky pastry. She took a sip of her café crème, having forgotten how small the coffee cups were in Europe. Large mugs of drip coffee had become the norm for her in medical school. She had practically needed an IV of caffeine to get her through some of those long nights.

"So, have you been doing some recreational driving since leaving Formula One?" she asked. She figured that the two of them had exhausted talking about her career. And she didn't know much about him now, other than that he used to drive cars.

Nicholas stared at her with an unreadable expression. "You really don't know, do you?"

Miranda put down her cup. "Know what?"

The waiter arrived just in time. "May I clear your plates?"

Nicholas nodded.

The waiter leaned in and tapped his watch. "And Nicholas, we open in fifteen. Just to give you time," he added surreptitiously.

Nicholas gave a brief nod of appreciation. "*Merci*."

Miranda sighed. "That was lovely. Thank you."

"You're welcome."

The atmosphere suddenly felt thick with words unsaid. Things Miranda wished she had followed up on. She felt a sudden urge to confide in him. To tell him everything. But she had barely done that with herself.

"So, you have to get going then?" she said instead.

Nicholas leaned back in the chair as if they had all the time in the world. "We still have a few minutes." He held out his glass towards her. "To old friendships."

"To new beginnings." She clinked her glass against his.

"I've just got to ask...did you ever go to the casino on New Year?" His tone was trepidations, as if worried about how she might reply.

The memory struck her like lightning. "No," Miranda answered, pulling a face in anticipation of his answer. "I'm hope you didn't either?"

He shook his head and smiled, visibly relieved. "We had stopped emailing at that point. And my life had gotten...busy."

She nodded. "I had figured as much." As she took time to look at him across from her, she realized his eyes weren't just brown as she gazed at him from over her glass. They were flecked with amber and even some thin lines of green. He had the skin of someone who had enjoyed luxuriating in the sun. And his smile?

Miranda's stomach flip-flopped.

That smile made her feel like she had her first crush all over again.

FOUR

Miranda

Ten years ago

M arkus was sitting at her kitchen table, wilted over like the blush and ivory peonies in the glass vase beside him. The two of them had been seated at that table for hours, just as they had countless times before. But this time, it was all different.

He had just explained why they should get back together *and* do long distance. To spare his feelings, Miranda pretended to consider his suggestion but knew deep down that it was never an option. A part of her couldn't wait to explore a new life, and another couldn't fathom leaving. He wasn't the reason she would miss Monaco, though.

"So? What do you think?" he asked her.

Miranda sighed and picked up one of the petals that had fallen onto the countertop. Their kitchen was mainly packed up, and they had nothing left except for the table, chairs, and the "going-away bouquet" that their neighbors had dropped off. It like the move was finally happening. In six days, she would be on a plane to start her new life.

"I think we gave it a perfect shot," she said gently. "Two years."

Markus' eyes sprang to life. "Exactly. Two years! Why throw that away just because of a move?"

Miranda shook her head. To her, Markus had been the perfect first boyfriend. He was attentive, thoughtful, and sweet. But she couldn't deny that she had fallen out of love with him months earlier. Pulling the plug on their relationship had been easier than she anticipated. Coping with him trying to get back together for the last few months had been hard. She had ended things well before the move was solidified. But he had latched onto it, seeming allowing it to give meaning to why she had ended things.

"I already told you, Markus, we're not together anymore because of more than the move. Things would have ended between us regardless," she said in as straightforward and kind a tone as possible.

His expression was pained. "You don't know that."

"I do."

The summer sun poured through the open window. In the distance, Miranda could hear the faint sound of the marina and cars driving below. It was a phenomenal apartment and she knew it would be hard to leave. In the springtime, their apartment had a view of the track for the Monaco Grand Prix. It was a big deal and her dads played it up, always throwing a party for the event. Not that they had a lot of family—it was just the three of them in Monaco. Chris had inherited the Monaco apartment from his aunt almost two decades earlier—his own parents were deceased. Kyle's family was from Canada and a few hours outside of Montreal by car. Although Miranda knew she was lucky, their setup was far from the glitz and glamour that sprang to mind when she told people it was where she was from.

Selling the apartment and moving to Montreal, where Kyle was from, would be a big adjustment. It was financially a good decision, her dads had explained to her, and an opportunity to try something new. After all—Christian had gotten his dream job at an art gallery in the heart of the city. The two of them had expressed their excitement to start new chapters of their lives and broaden her life experience. Most importantly, Miranda had said *yes*. They weren't the parents who made those decisions without her input. It had always been the three of them. It always would be.

Miranda walked over to the window and allowed the petal in her hands to take off with the wind. She told Markus she needed to continue packing, and after one last baleful look cast in her direction, he appeared to finally have gotten the hint, sulking as he walked out the door. Although she wasn't fully sure if he believed her when she told him they weren't getting back together, she couldn't have meant it more if she tried. He had been a great first boyfriend, but the spark had long faded. The more she got to know him, the more she felt their incompatibility would be a barrier to their relationship ever growing.

There was a knock at the door. When would Markus ever get the hint? "Did you forget something?" she asked.

"Uh, no..."

In front of her was Nicholas. Her shoulders dropped, and her hand flew to her mouth. "Oops! I thought you were someone else."

Nicholas gave her a lopsided grin. "May I come in?"

She gestured towards the empty living room, and Nicholas took a few steps inside.

"Wow," he said, looking around. "Weird."

Miranda followed him into the empty room. The wall sconces were the last reminders of their life there. "Weird indeed."

"How d'you feel?" he asked, turning around to face her. He crossed his legs and sat down in the middle of the room.

"I'm leaving in less than a week," she replied, sitting across from him. "How do you think I feel?"

Nicholas smirked. "You'll be back," he said with sureness. His floppy hair was falling over his eyes, and he had a way about him that was always easy to be around.

"Are you going to visit when you're a big star?" she asked.

He chuckled. "You never know. I'll take full offense if you don't come to see me race, though. Where are your dads, by the way?" He looked around at the nearly empty apartment.

"Saying bye to some friends. They'll be back soon."

"I want to say goodbye to them," Nicholas said.

Miranda knew he meant it. Her friend had always been like an extra member of their family. She felt butterflies swirling around her stomach, and she wasn't sure if it was nervousness about the move or him being there. Until recently, he had always been just Nicholas—her best friend, buddy, and pal.

Lately, something had changed.

She wasn't sure if it was him or her. Now, he didn't seem quite so goofy. In fact, she'd noticed that she started caring a bit more about how she acted around him. Other girls at their school asked if they were dating—they weren't. Was she planning on it? She wasn't sure how Nicholas would have replied if given the same question about her. But she was certain of what she hoped he would say.

He was perfect.

As soon as she realized her feelings for Nicholas, she ended things with Markus. The plan had been to tell Nicholas how she felt about him. But then her dads asked her about the big move. And she'd said yes.

Suddenly, telling Nicholas how she felt just wasn't right. The timing was all off. Why risk ending their friendship on such a potentially uncomfortable note? If he rejected her, and then she left Monaco, the ending would be so painful it would be almost unbearable. For some reason, she felt like she could only leave Monaco on a high note—that was the only way that leaving left doable. As long as things between her and Nicholas remained as they were. There was too much change already. That way, the door to come back was always open.

Besides, it was just a matter of time before everyone learned about what a catch Nicholas was, too. He was bound to get some stunning girlfriend the moment his racing career took off. Which it already was.

Even though he had told her the day before that he was signed to a team, she had a suspicion that things were moving in that direction. It was why when her dads had asked her about Montreal, Nicholas had flashed through her mind. But then she thought about his racing career. She didn't want to be the one left behind.

So she was moving to another country. Their worlds were on different paths.

"This doesn't have to be so depressing," Miranda said, her words cutting through the silence of the cavernous room. Without the furniture, her words sounded hollow. "It's not like one of us is dying."

Nicholas wrinkled his nose and pulled his knees into his chest. "I don't know when I'll see you again." His voice made her want to hug him. Instead, she took a seat on the floor and pulled her knees into her chest, too.

"Soon, I'm sure." But even Miranda was uncertain as she said it. When was she coming back?

"We'll stay in touch. Obviously," Nicholas added.

She nodded. "Obviously."

"How?" His tone sounded slightly anxious, which made her feel a bit better. If he thought this way, their friendship stood a chance.

"Emails, for sure. Phone calls..."

"I'll be traveling a lot this year for the races," Nicholas said. "Maybe I'll be in Canada."

"Maybe," Miranda shrugged. She hoped he would but knew he would be busy. "Honestly, I don't know when we'll see each other next."

Nicholas looked suddenly animated. "How about we meet back in Monaco in a year?"

41

Miranda pulled a face. "That *sounds* fantastic, but I'll still be finishing up school. I won't be done for another two years."

A look of comprehension dawned on him. "Right, right. Maybe two years?"

"When we're both eighteen?"

He nodded. "Yes."

"Where?"

"Outside the casino. With all the tourists."

"When?"

Nicholas paused. "The first of January. The New Year. At midnight!"

Miranda rolled her eyes. "Very dramatic," she said in a teasing tone. "But fine."

"I can't wait," he grinned.

She returned the smile and bit her lip. "Aren't you going to forget about me by then?"

Nicholas shook his head. "Don't worry. I could never forget about you."

Something warmed inside of her. "Me neither. For you."

He smiled. "Good."

"Good."

"Besides," Nicholas said. "The next two years are going to fly by. We'll see each other sooner than you realize. It'll go by in a minute."

"A Monaco minute," she said in a sing-songy voice. Although her tone was light, she couldn't help the ripple of fear that ran through her. Of the upcoming uncertainty. Of the emotions unspoken. And most of all, of everything she feared she might miss if she allowed herself to stay.

FIVE
Nicholas

Now

F ocus. Miranda was asking about work. He couldn't keep putting it off.

But then again, maybe he could. It was rare to run into someone who treated him so... *normally*. His life had hardly been normal from the get-go, what with being raised by a famous father—the esteemed Freddie Ridgeport, former racing driver and legend. But the last few years had been bumpy, to say the least.

When he first started in Formula One, his career had been hot, hot, hot. Every team wanted him after his first season. In his first year as a driver, he had even won the Monaco Grand Prix. It had been a legendary win. And he was pegged as *the* up-and-coming driver. Everyone wanted him. It was around that time that things started petering out between him and Miranda. Their emails gradually fell fewer and infrequently. He didn't recall if there was a set time when they had actually stopped. At the time, his life had been so busy and demanded all of his attention.

After his first year racing, he signed with a new team and things felt like they were taking off. Everyone had him pegged as a world championship contender. He didn't win the world championship that year. Or the year after. But the momentum from his first year career high carried him to a fourth year in the sport. For reasons he still struggled to understand, he seemed to have lost momentum and was

43

struggling to get on the podiums. His fifth year had been what he thought was a turning point—he was winning races and deemed to be a crowd favorite. He had come in third that season. But he got axed from his team for a younger driver and the last two years had been spent at a competitive team, to put it mildly. After an incident on the grid involving a crash, where everyone walked away, he was unceremoniously replaced with a rookie driver.

It had been a hard end to his racing career. For a while, he thought he would give up driving professionally once and for all. But that came with a whole other set of challenges he had not anticipated. His identity and world was wrapped up in racing. Without it, who was he?

He still didn't have a good answer.

The seven years he spent as a Formula One driver had been phenomenal. The best of his life. But he hadn't performed the way he had hoped. And when he was cut from his team, a void had been left in his life. That was three years ago. And it was no coincidence that for the last three years, he had felt lost.

Now, he was finally getting the chance he knew he needed.

When the Fairway team had reached out to him with the chance for a comeback, he felt it was almost too good to be true. Sure, younger, hungrier drivers were always waiting in the wings. That part was a worry. But he would be lying if he didn't think he as much of a killer as they were.

After three listless years, he was starving.

The press had been all over him since the news broke. It was perfect timing for his personal life to implode as well.

Now, here was Miranda. Acting towards him the way she had all those years ago. Back when they were just two kids without a care in the world with big dreams. Before life complications and expectations had gotten in the way.

"Nicholas? Did you hear my question?"

He returned his attention back to Miranda. "I'm sorry, my head was in another world."

Miranda laughed. "I just wanted to know a bit about your racing career. You were so passionate about it back when we were kids. And I saw a few of your early races. It seems like you had a successful career?"

Now was the time. Nicholas took a deep breath, bracing himself for everything to change. "I'm actually re-joining a Formula One team."

She looked interested. "As part of the team?"

"As a driver."

There. It was out there. Nicholas felt his breath catching in his chest. It would all be different now. It had been three years since he had been in a Formula One car. And he knew with certainty that everyone treated him differently when he was a driver.

And aspects of that were terrific. At the beginning of Nicholas' racing career, he felt practically invincible. He knew that he was fortunate.

But now, there was a lot to prove. In fact, a lot was hinging on this. Nicholas didn't like to think about it, much less talk about it. However, the whole racing community had said his career was up in smoke when he barely walked away from that crash involving three other drivers. Everyone chalked it up to him being at fault. It had been a brutal ending to a slowly stalling career.

Joining Fairway brought delirious excitement. But that joy had given way to anxiety. The tightness in his chest had been the first sign. His family doctor said it wasn't a heart condition, as he had feared. A heart condition was explainable and more manageable for him to comprehend. The trouble breathing had come later, although these things never happened in the car. The car was where he had complete and total clarity. It was when the cameras flashed, and the mic was put in front of him. He didn't know why these things bothered him now. They hadn't back then. In fact, he had started to feel a sense of low-grade panic most of the time.

He braced himself for her response. Would she ask for his autograph? Try to get him to take photos with her? There was something freaky about how differently people acted around him now. He waited for her response.

Nothing.

"I'm so happy for you, Nicky! That must be interesting," Miranda replied after a beat. She took a bite of the remaining breadstick and rested her chin on her hand.

Nicholas faltered. Had she heard him correctly? "Yes, I suppose it is."

"So, tell me more about what's changed in Monaco since I was last here," Miranda asked, her face lighting up. "I've missed it."

Nicholas' face burst into a smile. "I'd love to."

The next hour passed faster than a hot lap. Nicholas shared his experiences with Miranda about growing up in Monaco, about the antics of his former racecar driver, Freddie Ridgeport, and his mother, Charlotte Levant. He gave her the condensed version. After all, she surely remembered his unconventional route to finding his biological parents.

"Remember how much time we spent with your mémé?" Miranda asked. "I remember her so fondly."

Nicholas softened the way he did whenever someone spoke of his beloved grandmother and at the memories. "She's in her nineties now. Can you believe it? She's still living on her own. We always find excuses to pop in on her, bringing her groceries, meals, and things like that. But truthfully, she seems to be faring better than us sometimes," he laughed.

His grandmother had cheered him on throughout his racing career, especially at his lowest points. Back when he was young, she had been one of the first people he'd called upon finding out that he had a seat on a Formula One team. She had assured him that he could do it if he set his mind to it.

Miranda smiled. "She was kind. I remember my dads really liked her."

"And how are they?"

A pained expression flashed over Miranda's face, and she

looked away. "Um, it's just my dad, Kyle, and I now."

His eyebrows shot up. "Oh? I had no idea."

She fidgeted with the sleeve of her sweater. "It's fine. I've grieved."

Nicholas was surprised. He didn't know Miranda's fathers well, but from what he recalled, they had been the perfect picture of health. "How long ago?" he asked.

Her eyes dropped further. "A year."

Nicholas' eyes widened. "A year?"

Miranda met his gaze, and suddenly, he regretted his response. He could see the hurt in her eyes. "Like I said, I've grieved," she said carefully, unsure how he would reply.

Nicholas nodded. Although he hardly considered himself an expert on human emotions, he was pretty sure that wasn't how grief worked. "Okay."

"We didn't really advertise it," she said quickly, her words heavy but her tone detached. "The death, that is. Only a few people from Monaco knew about it from my dad, Kyle. He still keeps in touch with one or two people occasionally and isn't that active on social media either. He had written something online about the funeral though, which is how Markus found out about it."

He felt a tug at his heartstrings and shook his head. "Is Kyle coming with you?"

Miranda shook her head. "I think he found the idea of returning to Monaco without his spouse just too painful."

Nicholas paused for a beat, taking it all in. "And how about you?" he finally asked. "Has it been painful for you?"

Miranda frowned, and for a moment, Nicholas wondered if she would let him in on a secret. She looked up quickly and put on a smile. "I just got here. And I'm fine."

He could tell her smile was forced, but he didn't know her well enough to pry.

"I liked your dad, from what I remember of him. Both of them."

Miranda smiled as if in fond reminiscence. "He really loved watching racing. Especially the Monaco Grand Prix."

Nicholas felt himself perk up. "And you? Are you interested in racing these days?"

She wrinkled her nose. "It's been a while since I've thought about it. After that first year in Montreal, I decided I needed to really commit to my new life. I really focused on school. But I looked up you a few years ago and saw you'd...retired."

He appreciated that choice of words.

"Exciting to think you'll be back in Formula One," she continued. "I'm sure you'll do very well."

He felt his cheeks turning red. "I hope so."

"And what will life be like for you returning as a driver?"

He squirmed in his seat, wondering if now would be the time to tell her everything. About the esteemed seat he had just gotten signed for on a team where he could potentially win a world championship. And about why he was dreading the press.

"Nicky?"

"Yeah. Sorry," Nicholas replied. "It's pretty wild. I mean, I get to live my dream. I have a second chance to be the driver I know I can be." It wasn't a lie. But it certainly wasn't the whole truth.

She grinned. "That's so awesome."

"So, where are you staying while you're here?" he asked.

"A rental just outside of Monaco. This country is expensive," she said with a laugh. "I found a semi-affordable spot in La Turbie, about an hour walk from Monaco. But the clinic I'll be working at is here. Is just by Port Hercule."

"I'll bet your dad is going to come visit," he said, immediately regretting having brought up Kyle for a second time, based on Miranda's expression. "I mean—"

"—No, no. It's okay," she insisted. "Maybe my dad will come."

He could kick himself if he could. "I have a myriad of family dynamics that I struggle to navigate," Nicholas said, trying to lighten the mood. "You remember, I'm sure?"

Miranda looked more at ease almost instantly, and her eyes crinkled at the corners.

"I mean, how many people know that I was put up for adoption at birth, only to be adopted by my biological parents later?" he said with an incredulous laugh. It still felt surprising when he thought about it. "Not many people know the details. You and I met right when it all happened. Remember?"

"You were absolutely obsessed with racing, even back then. So competitive, too."

"I don't think you were much different," Nicholas said with a chuckle. "Not the racing part, but you were always the smartest in class. I knew you liked being number one."

"Not just being number one," Miranda countered. "It was the best coming in first, second, and third."

"Obliterating the opposition," Nicholas agreed. "You did that in school. Makes sense that you went to medical school."

Miranda shrugged. "I'm definitely not perfect. I've made some mistakes along the way."

"Like?"

"If I told you, I'd have to kill you," she said with a grin.

"I'll take my chances."

Miranda wrinkled her nose. "I had a client come in for blood pressure medication. I didn't read the notes beforehand. I was slammed. Instead, after looking at him and on first impression alone, I mistook him for a head injury referral I was seeing later that day. I asked him the severity of his concussion."

Nicholas pulled a face. "That's pretty bad. And probably not great for his blood pressure. But I'll bet I can beat you."

"Impossible. I almost died of embarrassment."

"A few weeks ago, a fan came up to me for a signature. They said it was 'for myself'. I spaced out and thought they said it was 'for Michael'. So, instead of signing it to their name, I signed the collector's edition that they had just purchased to Michael. It turned out they said it was 'for myself'—their name was Ashton."

Miranda pulled a face. "Yikes."

"And I was heading to a press conference. I would have bought them another hat but I needed more time. I could tell from their face that it took the wind out of their sails. And mine."

"Oh, that *hurts* just to think about!"

"I try not to," Nicholas replied. "So, do I win?"

"Never."

"Excuse me, *monsieur* and *madame*?" The waiter came up, startling both of them. "We are opening to the public in fifteen. I didn't want you to be alarmed."

He checked his watch. That morning had flown by. He wished he could ask the restaurant to stay closed for the afternoon, too, but it was too big of a request.

Miranda leaned forward after the waiter left them on their own. "I am still shocked to have run into you. And the way that we did. Straight out of a movie."

Nicholas felt his mouth twitch. "Straight out of a movie, indeed." He liked her. The attraction seemed mutual. It seemed effortless. Effervescent. And she was here for an entire year.

Unattached?

His eyes flitted to her hands. No ring. She hadn't mentioned anyone except Markus. But that was seemed to be more of an old-friends type of situation.

His mind raced back to his mother's words—something she had once told him. "You're the biggest romantic I've ever met, Nicholas. Make sure you save your heart for someone worthwhile. Someone who treasures it."

He had thought he had found that one particular person in the past. He had been sure of it. But alas, his judgment had been clouded by looks, beauty, and obvious attraction. And he was desperate for a distraction in his life at the time, which hadn't helped.

In his imagination, he was already carving out how they would make it work with Miranda. How he could fly back to see her in between races.

Get a grip, he reminded himself. *You always do this.*

"Well, shall we?" Miranda said, beginning to stand from the table.

As reality set in, the veil of anonymity from the restaurant was being lifted; Nicholas felt the moment's brightness dim slightly.

"So, where are you off to now?" he asked.

Miranda laughed. "Home. Or at least, where I'm staying for the next year. I've already emailed the rental office where I'm picking up my keys and let them know I am going to be late. I have to meet them now, just around the corner."

Nicholas nodded. What was he going to do for the rest of the afternoon? Reporters and media were swarming his apartment. This had been precisely the respite he needed. He wished that he could stay here forever. He just needed to keep out of the public eye for a day or two longer.

He stood up and passed Miranda's purse to her. "So, how do I get in touch with you?"

Miranda smiled, looking giddy. "I don't have my new phone number yet. Or my phone, for that matter. But you can email me. I'll let you know my number when I have my phone back. *If* I get it back."

Nicholas' heart pounded as passed his phone to her, allowing herself to send an email from his.

"Done," she said.

Now that he was checking his phone, he saw sixteen missed calls. And nearly twice as many text messages. His heart went from pounding to racing. *Shoot. This is going to be big.*

"Miranda, I think you should know..." He took a deep breath.

"What's up?"

"Some news is about to come out about me."

"What kind of news?"

Here it came. The big reveal. Nicholas swallowed the lump in his throat. "About my, uh, divorce."

SIX

Nicholas

Now

T here. Nicholas had said it aloud. The dreaded word—*divorce*. It hung in the air like a bad smell. The word he thought he would never have to say about his marital status. That word was reserved for other people. Not him.

Miranda frowned. "You're married?"

"In the process of getting a divorce," he quickly clarified, wincing at how it sounded.

"Oh," she pulled a sympathetic fact. "I'm sorry to hear that."

"Don't be," he said quickly. He kicked one foot against the other and looked down.

"Still," she said. "That's hard."

"Yeah. Uh, it's not been the easiest," he said quickly, trying to make light of it. "And it wasn't really much of a marriage. We did it on a whim. I wasn't thinking clearly. A few months passed, and I realized I had made a mistake..." He trailed off, wishing how things ended had been that simple and that his marriage could just be finished with similar ease.

She wrinkled her nose. "That's hard."

"The thing is, I'd love to see you again," he said determinedly.

Miranda paused for a beat. "I'd like that too."

He licked his dry lips, cursing the timing of everything. "My PR team and lawyer have asked me to be extra careful about my image. They don't want any stories coming out about me with other women during the divorce process, even if it's innocent. They worry about a story about me cheating on her, especially since we're not talking publicly about it all. In fact..." He didn't want to say it. He hated the way it sounded. "In fact, it was the other way around."

"Oh," she replied in a low tone. Miranda's eyes were filled with kindness.

He met her gaze. "So I've been advised by my lawyer not to have any appearances with, um, potential suitors." Why did his voice sound so cracked?

She looked amused. "Potential suitors?"

He felt his cheeks turning pink. "I mean, women who could be construed as potential suitors," he quickly clarified. Not that it made things much better.

"I see." The corners of her mouth were inching upwards, and her eyes sparkled.

He looked down again. Typically, he was an expert at this sort of thing—talking to beautiful women. Miranda made him feel like he couldn't string a sentence together.

"The thing is, this should blow over quickly. And when it does, it would be great to do this again," Nicholas tried for a final time.

"Sure," she said quietly. "I'd like that too."

"And if you could keep running into me at the airport between us," he said quickly, wondering if he was making any sense.

Her eyebrows shot up but she didn't ask any more questions.

"Anyways," he said quickly, trying to course correct. "I've really enjoyed this." Inwardly, he winced. How over-eager did he sound? This was like driving a race with precision only to spin out on the final lap.

She smiled, looking genuine. "Me too."

"So, I'll see you soon?" he added casually.

"Whenever. I'll be here!"

Her tone, warm and confident, was the epitome of cool. She made him nervous. Around her, none of his usual charm came with ease. He walked behind Miranda to the door, putting on his sunglasses and hat again. He peered around. Not a photographer in sight. Miranda smiled at him, and he felt his hopes rising. Maybe everything would work out.

"Welcome back to Monaco," he called out.

"It's good to be back," she called out as she walked away with a wave.

His heart began to speed up and he pulled his jacket collar up around his neck. Miranda was back. He walked towards his friend's apartment with a boost of energy in his step. After all, his own apartment was swarmed. He should have felt anxious. He should have felt annoyed. But he found himself biting down a smile.

Miranda was back.

SEVEN
Miranda

Now

F reshly out of a relationship? Starting a new career? Slightly beleaguered?

She wasn't sure if the description best fit her or Nicholas. Running into him had been the last thing she would have expected. But she couldn't have asked for a better start to her arrival. And that included her apartment showing.

"It's perfect," she gushed, looking around at her new home.

"You're sure?" the rental agent asked, barely masking their disdain at the small studio apartment. "We have others...of course, they come with a slight price difference."

She turned to him, not even put off by his candor. "It's perfect," she repeated herself.

Sure, the kitchen was tiny and lacked a proper oven, but she loved the colorful tile backsplash. The bed took up most of the living space but was covered with a cheerful quilt and art that looked like it had been inspired by the sea. It wasn't flashy or fancy, but it was clean.

Plus, the price was right.

The rental agent was already checking his phone. She thanked him for his time, and as she closed the door with her new keys in hand, she couldn't help herself grinning from ear to ear.

This was hers. Her own apartment.

Miranda would have called her dad if she had her phone, so she logged onto her laptop and, after a few attempts at connecting with the spotty Wi-Fi, she emailed him to let him know she was settled and safe. From her inbox, an email she'd marked as 'unread' stared at her, practically begging to be read. Again.

She couldn't help herself.

With one leg crossed over the other on the foot of her new bed, she felt practically transported to her old life from simply reading his name.

Connor.

As if in slow motion, she clicked to read it, feeling a little pang in her chest as if she hadn't gone over its contents a million times before.

Miranda. I miss you.
We all make mistakes. I promise to make it up to you.
Xo C

A spasm of concern rippled through her. After all, a part of her believed him. She wanted to. The date of the email had been ill timed—a week before her departure to Monaco. That email had her second-guessing her decision to leave.

"You've got to go," Avra had told her. "He abandoned you when your dad died."

"Not literally," Miranda replied, unsure why she felt the need to defend him.

Avra had rolled her eyes. "Babe. He might as well have. He emotionally abandoned you. He couldn't have been *less* there for you. And then to end things a few months after…"

Miranda had conflicting emotions about it all but knew better than to argue with Avra, especially about something her friend cared about. Things between her and Connor had ended in a murky, unclean way with him.

She had just gotten back to Montreal after completing her medical degree in Ireland. Connor had been another resident in the family medicine residency and they had gotten together a year into the three year program. Connor wasn't the type to be expressive with his emotions. He was cut and dry. In fact, when she first met him, she hadn't much liked him. He had been abrupt and a bit sharp in his demeanor. She later learned there was softness behind that hard shell. She had thought he would be a fantastic surgeon. It had surprised her that he was in family medicine—she later learned he wanted to do sports medicine as well. She thought it was fate when the two of them landed jobs at the same sports rehabilitation clinic the year earlier.

They lived together and had been together for three years when Chris had died. When her dad passed, Miranda had felt hollow. It felt like a blow at the end of a marathon. She was already numb, exhausted, and feeling slightly defeated after a gruelling few years. And she had just started her new job.

When she got the life-altering news, Avra had rushed to her side. Her dad, Kyle, was there every step of the way. She took two-weeks off of work to grieve.

During that time, Connor was practically nowhere to be found. Granted, he had just started his new job too, which is how Miranda made sense of it all. Shaken up, his absence went largely overlooked by her—but not by Avra. Connor had showed up in other ways, like being there at the funeral and sending her some texts through the day. But as Avra keenly reminded her, he had left early from the funeral to get back to work. And he never hung around longer than an hour or two. According to her dad, Kyle, Connor was a boy who didn't seem to know what he wanted—a career or a relationship.

When he asked her to move out a few months later, with his excuse being that they had drifted apart, she felt like her world had imploded. He had said that his priority was work.

In hindsight, she didn't know who she was more angry with—him for how he acted or herself for how she had reacted. At the time, she had been too mentally drained to argue. She was still felt numb from the death so his words had bounced off of her. She couldn't put up a fight. But there had been problems from early in their relationship—getting him to commit had been an ordeal in itself.

Now, she shut her laptop with a thud. It had been an adrenaline-fuelled last few months. And she'd been so eager to get through the pain without feeling it too much that she barely had a moment to catch her breath.

It was as if the exhaustion hit her in one fell swoop. She kicked off her flats and curled up in her new bed. It felt unfamiliar and smelled of a laundry detergent she didn't use. Faintly, she could hear the sound of other people living their lives in the adjacent apartments through the walls. She smiled—they sounded happy. The light poured in through the adjoining deck, which had a view of another apartment.

She allowed her heavy eyelids to fade shut, and for the first time in a long time, Miranda felt a knot in her chest unclench. Just a little bit.

***

Jet lag was in full force when Miranda opened her eyes, groggy and disoriented. She almost forgot where she was when she woke up. The sky was still dark but an amber glow came from the horizon line. Throwing on a jacket and boots, she left her apartment and took the winding roads all the way down to the water's edge where she sat along a rocky beach, watching the salty waves roll in and out with the tide. The sea, glimmering in the early morning sunlight, was already dotted with yachts and sailboats. The sky was slowly illuminating.

She was happy to have her feet firmly on the ground. Since she'd arrived in the Riviera, her head had been spinning. She had felt in another world. It felt good to be home.

She picked up a flat rock and threw it along the water, hoping to see it skip a few times. It plunked down, falling deep into the tide instead.

Before her move, Miranda had been working as a sports medicine physician at a sports medicine and rehabilitation clinic with Connor. She knew him in a way no one else did. His behavior hadn't come from nowhere—he had a profoundly complicated past with a turbulent upbringing and complicated family dynamics, which Miranda had used to excuse a lot of his own behaviour at the time. She truly believed him when he told her how sorry he had been, even though the apology had come too late.

Although she was scheduled to start her new job in a few days, they had left the invitation open for her to pop in sooner if she had time to get set up. Everything seemed to be a short distance by foot— one thing she particularly enjoyed but hadn't paid attention to when she lived there. Tears pricked at the pack of her eyes through the walk for a reason she couldn't allow herself to think about.

We were together for three whole years. What a waste.

She walked forty minutes to the clinic, using street signs and her memory to guide her. After all, she didn't have anything else to do that day. She was already settled. Besides, she loved getting a little lost.

Narrow roads curled up hills and alongside rocky walls, opulent buildings, and meticulous cobbled streets. She reminded herself that there was a reason she had come to Monaco and exhaled with a shudder. The knot in her chest remained. Her dad, Chris, had never particularly warmed to Connor while they had been together.

After her dad's death and her personal life's slow-motion implosion, she needed something new. She had needed an adventure. She needed to escape the city where everything reminded her of so much heartache. Now, here she was. Feeling homesick was no longer an option.

She followed the signs towards Port Hercules, Monaco's only deep-water port, and the nearest marker to the new clinic. The sun had fully peaked out of the horizon line, making the sea shimmer and glisten. The crescent shaped port had a street running along the parameter with angular towers perched alongside ancient-looking villas with balustrades and fancy gates. Her clinic was along here somewhere...

"Pardon me."

Miranda looked up to see she had walked right in front of someone. And the clinic. The name Monaco Rehabilitation was discretely listed in black and white ink on a cream-colored sign. She was here.

"I'm so sorry," she said quickly before moving out. She was prepared to head back home now—she'd only wanted to look at the clinic from the outside and see it in person.

"Miranda? Is that you?"

She turned around to see a man. Dark eyes and wavy hair tied back in a topknot. The smile gave it all away. That slightly over-eager smile.

"Markus!" He looked different from his photo on the clinic website. Taller. More self-assured. He certainly had grown up nicely.

He smiled at her as if thinking the same thing. "I thought you were popping in later this week. It's so nice to see you."

"I thought so, too. But, you know, jetlag," Miranda said, as if it explained everything. It was early and she felt like her brain was only semi-functional.

"Hopefully it has felt nice being back?"

Miranda laughed. "Yes. It's nice to be back. It's been ages."

"You heard our former classmate Nicholas Stefano is returning to the racetrack?"

Miranda beamed. "I heard."

He checked his watch. "You want to grab an espresso before I start?"

Suddenly, she felt exhausted. Perhaps it was the jetlag. "I have a lot of unpacking to do," she fibbed. "But it was nice seeing the clinic. And you! Thanks again for reaching out and suggesting the job."

He looked slightly put out but covered it with a smile. "No problem. I'll see you in a few days."

***

Those few days had come and gone. Although it hardly felt like it, Miranda was halfway through her first day at Monaco Rehabilitation. She was returning to the clinic after a break between clients, feeling slightly overwhelmed.

"Good walk?" the soft-spoken receptionist asked as she walked in.

Miranda nodded and smiled. Everyone at this clinic was polite. Although it was a rehabilitation facility, it felt more like a spa with its hushed music and cucumber water that they provided to everyone who passed through the sleek glass doors. The atmosphere was a tad different from where she was used to working, back at the clinic with several colleagues, including Connor. Her old clinic was utilitarian and unglamorous, but they had one of the best track records for treating serious sports-related injuries. Athletes sought her out. Since beginning there, she had worked with professional marathoners, soccer players, boxers, and swimmers regularly for years since they flocked to the best places for treatment of their injuries. In hindsight, it was no surprise that her first-class experience and Monaco passport made her a shoo-in for working at Monaco Rehabilitation.

She made her way to her brand-new office past the reception desk. Calming jazz played over a sound system, and the air smelled of fresh laundry. This was nothing like the old clinic back in Montreal. Back there, she had worked wherever there was free office. Here, everything was shiny and new. She had an office all to herself with a little nametag on the door, which read *Doctor Thatcher.*

"Knock knock?" Doctor Elbar appeared at her door. He was the clinic director and the one who had hired her after Markus had made the recommendation. "How are you enjoying your first day?"

Miranda shifted in her seat. He was a chiropractor, although no longer practicing, and oversaw the operations of the clinic he'd founded. Markus was his nephew and responsible for client outreach, soliciting clients from various sports teams and outside sources.

"My first day is going great, thank you," she said. It was true. She'd felt slightly panicked at the note-taking software and billing systems they had in place—both new to her. She would learn soon enough.

Doctor Elbar leaned against the door frame. "You know, you're our only sports medicine physician on staff taking clients. We have two more sports medicine physicians who aren't taking on new clients, an osteopath, three chiropractors, a podiatrist, a myriad of physiotherapists, and now you. We have a client who is looking for some support from someone with your background. It would involve sessions here but potentially working with them on the road. I know it's your first day and all..."

"It's an honor to be asked," Miranda managed, not wanting to appear ungrateful.

He looked at her expectantly.

"I think I would need to meet the client first," she said thoughtfully. "But I'm not opposed to the idea."

Doctor Elbar clapped his hands together. "Wonderful. By the way, we do this all the time—if a professional athlete needs one of our clinicians on the road with them, we do what we can to accommodate that." The doctor looked pleased with himself. "For a reasonable fee, of course," he added as an afterthought.

Miranda bit back a smile. "Thank you, Doctor Elbar. I really appreciate the opportunity. I look forward to meeting the client."

"Very well. And you're settling in otherwise?"

"So far so good!" she said. And it wasn't a lie. It also wasn't the whole truth. Over the last few days, she felt homesick. She missed her dad, Kyle. She missed Avra. She missed parts of her old life. She had started to feel lonely in her apartment late into the evening. And she still didn't have her phone to help her connect with everyone back home. Was she already regretting her decision? That it had been poorly thought out and a reaction to everything that had happened?

No, she could never tell anyone that.

"It's going perfectly," she said again, less to Doctor Elbar and more to herself.

Later that afternoon, Miranda saw her first three clients for initial assessments. She arranged her desk at the end of the day. On it, she had placed a picture of her with her dads back when they all lived in Monaco. It still didn't feel possible to her that he was gone when she looked at the picture. He looked young and healthy, with stubble and a mischievous smile. And her other dad seemed very different. In the photo, Kyle was happy—grinning from ear to ear. His sandy hair was sun-kissed, and there was an air of ease about him. The man she had kissed goodbye at the airport was strained with a permanent furrow between his brows. As a doctor, she certainly didn't expect him to bounce back right away. He was grieving. But she couldn't have anticipated the toll it took on her to see him hurting.

She looked around her unfamiliar surroundings, wondering if she shouldn't just stuff the items back into her purse, tell Doctor Elbar it wouldn't work out, and get on the soonest plane back to her loved ones.

Out of idle curiosity and a little homesickness, she typed the name Connor's name into her search feed and waited. Almost immediately, his profile burst to life on her laptop—new photos of him on his social media and...who was that? An unfamiliar-looking blonde was cuddled beside him in almost half his recent images.

Miranda felt a pang in her chest, making it hard to breathe. *Who is that? Who is she?*

Her office phone rang. She picked it up, expecting to hear the voice of the receptionist. Or perhaps Doctor Elbar.

"Miranda speaking," she answered in clipped tones.

"Hey, it's me."

She froze. Her heart felt like it was about to explode upon hearing his voice. Was she hallucinating?

He continued. "Connor, I mean. It's me, Connor. I heard you moved back to Europe? Did I hear that right?"

She wanted to hang up right away. But another part of her was gripped, unable to tear the phone away from her ear. The two of them had not been on talking terms since the breakup—more specifically, since he had asked her to move out. Avra had told him to stay away from her with a ten-foot pole.

But Connor was Connor.

Why was he calling? How did he find out where she was working? "Why are you calling me, Connor?" she managed, feeling proud of herself for maintaining a slightly chilly tone.

"We need you here. I need you here. I messed up."

Miranda felt like the wind had been knocked out of her.

"Hello? Miranda? You still there?"

"I'm still here," she replied, her voice ice cold. She didn't know how she felt. Her heart had been thrown around and torn apart within the last year.

What about the blonde? What about those photos? There were muffled voices in the background that Miranda could faintly make out as being from her colleagues.

"Yeah. We're having a major crisis with intake," Connor continued. "We've got a soccer player with a head injury. He said he only wants to work with you based on some treatment you provided to his teammate."

The realization of what she thought Connor meant versus what he actually meant dawned on her. He didn't need *her*. The clinic needed Doctor Thatcher. She shut her eyes, feeling like the world's biggest idiot. Yet again.

"How did you find out where I work?" She fought through the crack in her voice.

"I Googled you," he said proudly. "You're on their website. I was stunned to read you're in Monaco."

She said nothing and tried to modulate her breaths. Deep breath in, slow breath out.

"We do miss you here," he continued. "It's not the same without you. I miss you," he added, sounding more like he meant outside of their working relationship.

Miranda felt her heart pulling in a million directions. Up. Down. Up. Down.

"Look, I was thinking—" he said.

Miranda's breath caught in her throat. She hated that she still felt something when she heard his voice.

There was a crash on the other end. "Oh, shoot. Miranda. Look, I've got to go. Something came up—"

The distraction in his voice was evident, and Miranda knew there was no use prying. He was gone. The conversation was as good as done.

"Bye, Connor. And please... don't call me again," she added for good measure, feeling satisfied with how she handled it.

But she didn't feel proud of the emotions that welled within her as she hung up. *Was Connor telling me that he misses me?* She felt her hopes soar just a little bit, thinking about how good it would feel to hear him acknowledge how badly he had messed up. How much easier life would be if she was able to go home to see Avra, hang out with her dad, and mend things with Connor. A small part of her craved the simplicity. The nostalgia. The way things used to be. Back when her family was still together. And back when she didn't feel so alone.

EIGHT
Nicholas

Now

" Nicholas, what did I tell you? The balloons go on each side of the door."

Freddie Ridgeport wasn't yet dressed for the party, wearing a sun-faded long-sleeved polo. Nicholas' father loved to tease him with mock exasperation. He held out a cup of coffee, which Nicholas gratefully accepted.

His divorce had been made public. And already the headlines were taking aim. It was hard for him not to feel affected and the negative press brought him back to some of his darker moments when he had been let go by his team.

"The balloons look better like this," Nicholas retorted in deadpan tones, knowing fully well that the slightly deflated clump of them that sat on the terrace looked less than celebratory.

"If your mother thinks it's ugly, I'm blaming it all on you." Freddie held up his hands as if to admit defeat. There was an intentional lightness to his father's tone, which Nicholas appreciated. Everyone knew how much today mattered. And no one knew better than Freddie, who remained a legendary racer that drivers continued to look up to.

Big shoes to fill, Nicholas couldn't help himself but think.

As he continued to decorate for the party, he allowed himself to briefly entertain the best-case scenario, and the corners of his mouth lifted. He would be starting his new season as a driver for the Fairway team within a few weeks—the opportunity of a lifetime. A chance to rewrite his history. A chance to have the legacy he'd always wanted. He couldn't mess this up.

A spasm of worry hit him right in the chest.

This upcoming season mattered more than ever before. Because if Nicholas didn't manage to perform at the level that was required, he would be axed from the team. He had a one-year contract. And then what? A part of him wondered why he'd even agreed to this. It put a lot of pressure on him. But then, who was he without racing? This was his comeback.

The experience of leaving a sport he'd loved his whole life without accomplishing what he felt capable of had left him with a pervasive feeling of unease for years. Now was his chance to rewrite his history.

What if you fail?

Keep putting up balloons, he told himself.

In less than three hours, his closest friends and family hailing from Monaco and various small towns that sat like jewels along the French Riviera would arrive for the well-timed gathering. It would be the first party in the newly acquired Ridgeport family home. This ancient villa sat along the craggy coast of the Mediterranean Sea in Monaco. And for him, it was the perfect chance for him to spend more time with Miranda. He had sent her an email and invited her.

"It will be great," he said aloud to himself. *It had to be.* Everything necessary in his life felt eggshell fragile today, although no one would know it by looking at him. No one knew that beneath the calm confidence that he portrayed, he was just barely treading water. How could the pressure not be getting to him? How could those comments on fan forums, the ones he swore he would never look at again before returning the following week, not affect him? The son of a legend. The chance to rewrite his ending in a sport that he loved. The pressure was immense. Sometimes, he felt he was about to explode.

Pop!

"I think you've overdone it with that balloon," Freddie noted. "Everything okay?"

Nicholas realized that he was holding the now-broken balloon with all his might. "Great," he fibbed.

"If you say so."

Nicholas began again, being careful not to overfill the balloon this time. "Done!" He tied the final balloons with a flourish and stood back to admire his work. They fell limply against the white stucco house's exterior, swaying in the cool salty breeze. He squinted as he tilted his head to the side. It didn't look *quite* like the photo that his family had sent around for inspiration.

"Well, this looks like quite the professional job. You've got the magic touch," Freddie said, his mouth twitching at the corners, thinly disguising his snorts of laughter. "In addition to this beauty..." he continued, gesturing at the heaps of balloons that looked more like sad bouquets of wilted flowers. "...we've got an oven that stopped working at the last minute, about a million canapés that need to be heated, and a few last-minute cancellations, but *thankfully*, we have the decor to bring it all together."

Nicholas and Freddie looked around at the attempt they had made and burst into laughter, giving him a momentary reprieve from the butterflies that danced in his stomach.

"Give me a half-hour," Nicholas insisted, his perfectionist streak flaring. "It will be perfect. Who canceled earlier, by the way?"

"Some of your mémé's friends," Freddie said, referring to Nicholas' grandmother.

Inwardly, Nicholas breathed a sigh of relief. At least it wasn't some racing bigwigs he hoped to meet with. As long as the right people showed up, Nicholas felt he could keep the feeling that he would explode under wraps. With all the adrenaline pumping through his blood as he waited to see how the upcoming racing season went, he really needed a friend.

Don't forget you have to return that call to the divorce lawyer. He shoved the thought from his mind. How had he been so naive? How did everything in his life get so messy?

"Boys, what a sight," Charlotte said as she walked onto the patio. His mother was already dressed for the "intimate" soiree. According to Charlotte, just "a few" of Nicholas' friends had been invited because there was no occasion too small for a party, including the need for some simple distraction from the headlines he was facing.

Nicholas anticipated a guest list of no less than one hundred.

Charlotte checked her watch. "We've got to be party-ready in two hours." A flicker of worry crossed her face, but she said nothing. Leave it to Charlotte Ridgeport to remain calm and collected with so much to do in so little time.

Nicholas brushed a bead of sweat from his forehead. The golden sunlight glowed over the entire French Riviera that late afternoon. Even in cooler months, it was still pleasant to be outside. Like all the days in the weeks leading up, there wasn't a cloud in the sky.

Nowhere I'd rather be, Nicholas thought. Monaco was home.

It was the first party the family was having about their new villa. The manor had needed extensive repairs when his parents made the purchase and had lovingly restored the old estate to its former glory. The ornate iron railings along the patio gleamed after years of neglect. The deep cracks in the old stucco had been filled. Ancient plumbing had been overhauled. The overgrown garden had been tamed. The only thing about that house that didn't need any work was the view.

"I'll never tire of it," Charlotte said, walking over to where Nicholas stood as if reading his mind. "Do you think you'll miss it when you're off traveling the world for another year?"

Her eyes twinkled, and her cheeks were flushed from running around getting everything ready. It was embarrassing to admit, if only to himself, that he had missed his family when he was away in the early days of his career. But he certainly wasn't about to get sentimental. That wasn't the style for any of his family, especially with a party about to be underway, so he smiled and said nothing as the two of them looked out at the view.

Leave it to his mother to throw a party to distract him from the chaos in his life. Charlotte had once confided to him how scared she had been about returning to Monaco, worrying that neither he nor Freddie would forgive her for leaving years earlier. The three of them had been a family ever since. It hadn't been without bumps in the road, but they now treaded on smooth terrain for the most part.

"Chantal was asking about you."

The voice made Nicholas look up from where he was making a mess of tape and balloons along the balustrade. Marco wandered onto the patio with the ease of someone who lived there. His friend sported newly bleached hair, contrasting against heavily tanned skin, which he worked on at the beach on the weekends. His hair changed approximately every two weeks, and it was the only inconsistent trait about him.

Not that hair was on Nicholas' mind. He ran his hand through his own as he swallowed a lump in his throat. Just mentioning her name made his chest tighten...and not in a good way.

"You're still in touch?" Charlotte asked, her voice a few octaves higher than normal.

Marco cracked up. "I'm just kidding. Rumour around Monaco is that she's sporting a new ring, though. On a significant finger."

"She's engaged?" Nicholas balked. Just her name felt like a blow to the chest. Chantal. Just because it ended as quickly as it started didn't mean his emotions had fizzled entirely, too. It was complicated. Their divorce wasn't yet finalized.

And no one knew the truth.

Chantal had come into his life when he needed her most. Beautiful, lively, and full of confidence and charisma, it wasn't hard to see why he had fallen for her. When the two of them met at a beachside bar, he had been feeling particularly lost. He hadn't had a clue about his next steps in life. She had been the distraction he had needed. They had quickly fallen in love and gotten married.

He later learned it was never love for her. It was lust.

When he had found her and his best friend, it crushed him. Sure, he and Chantal had gotten together quickly but thought it was real. There hadn't been any indication of her wanting to end things. Or her attraction to his friend. But then again, maybe he hadn't been looking. In hindsight, he felt like an idiot for the whole relationship. He had thought there was had been something special between them. He wasn't sure what had hurt more—the heartbreak or the betrayal.

It had been a huge surprise when Chantal had asked him to come to London a few days earlier. He figured she would apologize. He would never be able to reconcile what had happened but his ego had been wounded. And even though he hated to admit it, he really had loved her.

But it had been a very different kind of conversation from what he had expected. With tears of mixed joy and concern in her eyes, she had tenderly held her stomach.

It wasn't his.

Nobody else knew. He hadn't told his friends or family. And that had been all the information he had needed to know from her. He packed up and left the meeting almost as soon as he had arrived. Running into Miranda at the airport on his way home was the last thing that he had expected. And why he didn't want anyone to know about his flight. He wasn't even divorced yet.

He didn't like to think about that morning; he had returned to their apartment early from practice. And he hadn't spoken to her or his old racing buddy ever since—his former friend and now rival. Serge Versuvio.

Nicholas' other friend Liam arrived just in time to redirect the conversation.

"There you are! I knew you'd make it," Marco said, clasping his friend.

Liam's eyes crinkled at the corners as he made the rounds, giving everyone a hug. His two best friends had the same primary interest as him: racing. Luckily, there was minimal competition between them as their interests varied. Marco was a mechanical engineer and worked on cars in various motorsports. Liam was seeking an aerodynamicist job and had just returned from Paris, where he had just finished his education.

The three of them had been tight for over a decade and become close when Miranda had gone to Canada with her family. Nicholas had first become buddies with Marco after Marco stepped in and helped him fight off some bullies. Nicholas was small in stature as a kid. Marco, luckily, had always had a sturdy build and had been the friend Nicholas had not just wanted but the one he had needed. Liam came into their friend group a year later after they met on the karting track. They had been practically family ever since.

Nicholas had been working towards becoming a Formula One driver since he was nine. Although he had achieved that goal, it turns out that simply being on the grid wasn't enough for him. He had to make a lasting impact on the sport—and end that chapter on his own terms. After his adoptive parents died and he first moved in with Freddie, his biological father, racing helped them bond. After all, Freddie was a retired racing legend himself. Nicholas had always had laser focus—probably genetic, he had determined, considering Freddie's demeanor.

But that perfectionism had changed with the pressure he had endured over the years. In his early career, his perfectionistic streak made Nicholas an excellent driver. After he was cut from his team, his entire identity was thrown into question. Who was he without racing? Without vying for a number one spot on the podium? In his last few months, his determination to succeed with this new venture had turned into angst. Sometimes, Nicholas felt he could barely stand the feeling of *not* knowing what the season held. It was enough to make him feel a crushing, gnawing sensation in his chest, making it hard to breathe...

Everything is fine, he told himself, as he often did. *Everything will be perfect.*

No, it's not.

Liam had the most relaxed attitude of the trio and mostly just looked forward to the clubs they frequented on weekend nights and his latest date. His friend simply had no interest in finding love or "the one" at such a young age.

Sometimes, he wished he could be more like Liam.

"Who is coming tonight?" Liam asked, sitting on one of the lavish wrought iron benches.

Nicholas listed off the usual crowd they'd grown up with and some of the racing crowd whose company he enjoyed. "And then, uh, Miranda."

Liam's brow furrowed. "Miranda? Miranda, who?"

He felt his heartbeat quicken. He hadn't told his friends or family about running into her yet. He didn't know why he hadn't. It seemed silly to have kept it a secret. Not that it was a secret, he figured; he just hadn't wanted their lines of questioning.

"From school."

Marco's eyes lit up. "Not *Miranda* Miranda?"

He nodded. "That's the one. It's no big deal. We ran into each other the other day."

Marco grabbed his friends' shoulders and shook them. "Bro— you're set! I'll start planning the wedding."

Nicholas pulled away from his friend and laughed. "I'm not even divorced yet."

Marco swatted the air. "Ah, it's just a detail."

"Yeah, who says I'm even ready to date anyway."

"How was seeing her?" Liam asked.

"Fine," he said, wanting to change the conversation from his dating life. Not that the two of them were *dating*. He just had to ensure his friends didn't embarrass him tonight.

"Did I hear you mention Miranda?" Charlotte asked, walking out of the house with a vase of flowers. "Not *Miranda* Miranda?"

"She's back!" Marco shouted. "When was the last time you saw her?"

Charlotte appeared thoughtful. "It's been years. Did she mention how her dad's have been? I heard one of them was ill."

Nicholas looked down. He felt awkward mentioning her dad's

death in the crowd. "I think I'll finish getting ready," he said, making his way inside.

He still had a room at his parent's house even though his apartment wasn't too far away. Once secluded, he scrolled through his phone, letting his worry melt with each swipe.

The last time his family had gotten excited about a prospective date, it had been Chantal. A whole year earlier. That felt like a lifetime ago. Now, he was sorting out the details with the divorce lawyers. He would laugh if he didn't feel so stung. He thought he had finally gotten it all—the second chance at a career and the girl.

Now, he had crushing anxiety at his parents' house and a divorce in the works. He could laugh if he didn't feel so sorry for himself. The last year had chipped away at his confidence, and he was left doubting his confidence and intuition.

Tonight might be the moment he needed to change course. Maybe tonight was exactly what he needed. A chance to prove to himself that he was still fun, young, and a contender to be a world champion—a winner.

NINE

Miranda

Now

S he had her phone! It felt like she was finally reunited with a long-lost love. She'd used the landline in her rental apartment to call the airport every day since she landed, and, as luck would have it, it finally turned up. As soon as she had picked it up, she texted her dad, Avra, and with a little bit of thought, she sent Nicholas a quick message on the number he had emailed her.

He had replied back almost instantly, inviting her to a party at the Ridgeport's new house that evening.

She didn't know what she was more excited about—the phone or the party.

She stared at herself in the mirror of her apartment. She was wearing a new outfit that she had bought before the trip. Her hair was pulled up in a clip, and she wore wide-leg champagne-colored pants and a matching halter-neck top that tied at the back.

She was invited to a *soirée*, as her dad would have called it. A crease formed between her brows as the memory of him surfaced. Chris had always loved events—the bigger and splashier, the better. He was—*had been*—the life of any party. It felt surreal that he wasn't here. She stared at herself in the mirror and blinked back a few tears. Distracting herself from her emotions, she zeroed in on smoothing the crease on her pant leg.

You're fine, she told herself and took a few deep breaths.

Everything in her new place was set up. She had provided her deposit to the rental company and had already unpacked all her belongings.

After getting her phone at the airport, she'd spent the earlier part of the day getting ready at her place, which she determined had to have been renovated in the sixties. It had a small rectangular balcony off the main room where she had sipped her coffee that morning. Although the whole place was rectangular and plain, she loved it. Her apartment had a small entryway, bathroom, and a little kitchen that opened onto the balcony, and the living room and bedroom were in the same room. It was cozy, to put it generously.

Her clothing barely fit in the closet, and the armoire was already there when she arrived. She still had an entire suitcase left to unpack.

There was a frameless rectangular floor-length mirror in the sparsely decorated rectangular hallway, where she now checked her appearance before heading out that evening for Nicholas' party. She couldn't wait to add her personal flair to the place.

With a few spritzes of perfume, Miranda grabbed her keys, her phone, and her purse. She preferred walking as much as she could. Setting off by foot, she made her way through the winding roads, breathing in the fresh air and feeling a chill run through her body as she made her way to the Ridgeport's new villa. When she was last in Monaco, the Ridgeports had lived in an apartment.

As she made her way through the streets of Monaco, memories surfaced—ones she hadn't thought about in a decade. Passing by the glamorous and iconic opera, she was reminded of the birthday when her dads had taken her. She felt a pang in her chest, looking at the stairs and remembering how Chris had offered his arm for her to hold, since she had worn heels for the first time and teetered with each step.

She continued her walk, noticing how some of the stores were the same. The cafe where she went in the morning with her dads was still there, with black and white chairs and ferns hanging in the windows. A part of her wished she felt happy—those had been lovely memories. Good times. But she felt a shiver run up her spine instead.

Continuing on, Miranda soon found herself at the end of a nondescript dead-end road, gasping for breath as she walked up the narrow street. She was grateful to have worn comfortable flats. She checked her phone to double check that she had typed in the right address. Was this the right place? Her phone said she had arrived. There was a modern, peach-colored apartment to her right and a wall with vines hanging off of it to her left. No house in sight. As she glanced around, she saw a tiny path that was hidden behind more bushes some fencing. The brick path led up a small hill to a pale stucco building with balustrades, bright pink bougainvillea, and a large iron gate. This had to be the place.

She was buzzed in and as she stepped into Ridgeport villa, she thought it was straight out of a Rivera living magazine. Cream colored and perched on a hill with views of the Mediterranean Sea. She took a final deep breath as she braced herself for a blast from the past.

***

The Ridgeport villa was a grand, old-world manor with warm, modern touches. The Versailles parquet hardwood gleamed beneath her feet, the white walls surrounding them were ensconced in luxurious molding, and the chandeliers sparkled from the high ceilings. Waiters in crisp white shirts and black vests circulated with silver trays of champagne and cheerfully colored mixed drinks. This felt more like a fancy wedding than a "simple party," as Nicholas had sold it to her.

A whole hour had inched by. The woman across from her, a former classmate she vaguely remembered, sounded exactly like the kind of person Miranda sometimes wished she could be. "So I'm going to travel the world for a year just to find myself, you know?" Her old peer sipped champagne nonchalantly and looked without care in the world as a diamond-encrusted anklet dangled off her bony foot.

Miranda laughed and smiled, nodding as if she too had the luxury of "finding herself"—whatever that meant.

"...and then I'll go to Australia because you know, everyone should spend at least a year of their life in another continent, you know?"

Miranda smiled tightly as her phone buzzed from her pocket. She pointed at it apologetically as the screen illuminated. "Sorry, I need to take this. I'll be right back," she feigned.

She made her way to one of the marble-clad powder room before pressing decline to the telemarketer before checking to see if Avra would answer her phone. She dialed, and it immediately went to voicemail.

What's the use of having a best friend on standby if she didn't pick up when I need her?

Leaving the powder room, Miranda immediately felt eyes on her. A tall and lanky young man she had never seen before rushed up to her, slightly sloshing some of his drink onto the terracotta tile flooring.

77

"You're new here." The man had a British-accent and he poked her shoulder with his free hand as if making the most astute observation in the world.

"Kind of." She certainly felt new to Monaco. Everywhere she looked, it felt like an unfamiliar face was peering at her with curiosity. A part of her felt homesick for her old life.

"I moved here a few years ago," the man said. "Best place in the world."

As he began to talk about cryptocurrency with fervor, smelling of too much cologne and appearing to enjoy the sound of his voice, she managed a smile while looking around for an out, but everyone around her seemed wrapped up in their conversations. Truthfully, she didn't even want to be at this party. According to Nicholas, this party was supposed to be *the* event of the year—she hadn't been sure if he was kidding or not over the messages. It was also her first time to "reunite with some familiar faces" now that she was returning home. It was strange how she barely recognized a single person.

Maybe coming here was a mistake. The thought popped into her mind before she could stop it as the man across from her continued to talk. *You don't know this place anymore.*

As the man continued to talk, Miranda was captivated by her surroundings. The ivory walls had square moldings and a limestone fireplace in the living room off of the foyer. The black-and-white marble tile floors led to a sweeping staircase with a grey runner up to the second floor.

Where was Nicholas? She had been here for fifteen minutes and still hadn't once seen him. Or any of his family, for that matter. She would try to find them to say a quick hello and goodbye before making her leave.

She couldn't help but want to look up plane tickets to head back home. Her real home. With Avra, her dad, Kyle, and her favorite coffee shops and snowy winters. Before she left Montreal, her dad had insisted she would enjoy Monaco. That it was where she was from and would always be her home.

Now that I'm here, it doesn't really feel like home anymore, Miranda thought.

"Right, well, thanks for the crypto tips," she managed as the man across from her paused between ideas. "I'm just going to run to the ladies quickly..."

As she made her escape through the crowd, she was able to

pick out a few familiar faces here and there. Hadn't she gone to school with a few of them?

She made her way up the grand staircase, where there was a quieter space on the mezzanine landing. Awards and trophies lined the hallway as she swiveled her head around, taking it all in.

She tried to call Avra again and exhaled in relief as she heard her friend's familiar voice.

"Spill. I want to hear all the details," Avra said as soon as she picked up.

Miranda turned up the volume to drown out the sound of the music that thumped in the background. She could hear the crunch of pretzels being eaten into the receiver. A wave of longing hit her. What she wouldn't give to be back with her friend. Suddenly, Miranda yearned to return to Avra's downtown condominium, where they could order takeout and talk until the early hours.

"No details. Honestly, I don't know anyone here. It's weird being back. I think I'm going to head back to my apartment."

"No way are you quitting early!"

Miranda smiled. Avra was constantly pushing her out of her comfort zone. Her friend was always the one to make them reservations at new restaurants or push her to go to parties. Miranda enjoyed being on the sidelines rather than in the limelight. It worked perfectly for their friendship, considering that Avra's career as a family lawyer was taking off. Avra shined with her sparkling personality, persuasive way of speaking, and ability to win arguments. In fact, it was Avra who had insisted that Miranda take the opportunity to work in Monaco for a year. The two of them told each other everything.

"You're locked in for a year there," her friend continued. "So many people would do anything to be in your shoes."

Would they? She thought about her dads and about the year she had. She sure didn't feel all that lucky.

Avra seemed to read her mind. "I didn't mean—"

"—I know," she quickly replied.

Of all the people who knew how brutal Chris' death had been for Miranda, it had been Avra. Her friend knew how absurd Miranda had felt when deciding to move to Monaco after reading the request from her dad in his will that she come back for the car.

A car? *A car*???

Not to mention it was a car she hadn't seen in years. A car she frankly didn't care about. Because he was gone. He wasn't coming back. What use was an old car?

She had relinquished herself to coming back to Monaco for the car. The job was a bit of an accident. She remembered the moment a few weeks earlier when she had gotten the email that changed everything. She skimmed over those words and feeling delirious, she was so pleased, and then guilty for feeling glad. *Your application for the position of staff physician (sports medicine) at Monaco Rehabilitation has been accepted...*

Excitement and the desire for something new had fueled her to say yes. But those high emotions were quickly followed by fear. Applying to Monaco Rehabilitation had been a distraction from her pain. Markus had reached out to her after hearing about her loss. As they talked, he told her about Monaco Rehabilitation and they were hiring. It had gotten her thinking. It was a one-year contract for a once-in-a-lifetime opportunity. And a chance to hopefully feel closer to her late dad.

Right now, she couldn't feel more alone.

She figured that even if she just focused on the career aspect of the journey and nothing more, it was the best sports rehabilitation facility of its kind, so surely it wouldn't be a waste of time. Athletes from all over traveled for treatment there. And they had chosen *her*. She still felt a frisson of disbelief when she thought about it.

"Are you even listening to me?" Avra's voice brought her back to the present, back to the party.

She looked around with a trill of butterflies in her stomach.

"Of course..." she fibbed.

"Well, I was just saying how I really think everything will work out with his job. And being back in Monaco."

A stab of emotion threatened to bubble up. It didn't even begin to cover Miranda's worry about the actual task ahead of her—the job she had haphazardously applied to and shockingly been accepted to. What if she couldn't deliver? What if she couldn't help people the way she had in the past? She had applied on a whim, at Avra's urging no less, after everything in her life felt like it was falling apart. It never occurred to her that she would actually get the job. But here she was.

"For sure," Miranda agreed. "If I can make it in this job and start making a name for myself, then maybe I can start my own clinic," she heard herself saying. Her own clinic. That sure felt like a nice idea.

"Exactly. Keep that in mind—you could have your own practice at the end of all this. Or, who knows, maybe you'll want to stay in

Monaco—"

"—I'm just here for one year," Miranda cut her friend off. "One year."

Her last year had been a complete roller coaster of emotion. She was doing her best to push it all aside. It didn't help that when she looked over the balustrade overlooking the party, couples looking in love seemed to be everywhere. Miranda suppressed a sudden wave of nervousness as she looked around at her opulent surroundings and the people who seemed so at home in it.

I'm out of my depth here.

As if reading her thoughts, Avra piped up. "Hey, you've got this."

"I don't know how I got myself into this situation."

"Hey, snap out of it! You're a kickass doctor trained with the best, that's why!"

Miranda wished she could hug Avra through the phone.

She thought about the contract she had reviewed with the clinic earlier that day. She was now officially on staff, albeit on contract, at Monaco Rehabilitation, where she would be working with the most exclusive clients.

But if she was being honest, she couldn't care less about the select clients they boasted. That hadn't been the draw for her. When Markus had mentioned the job, she desperately needed something new. She needed a change. She needed to leave Montreal. There were too many ghosts following her around—wondering if she would run into Connor or if something would trigger the memory of her dad.

The job was a breath of fresh air.

And she had desperately needed *not* to work at the clinic where she had initially been.

Looking around, she felt a pang of anxiety—none of this had been part of the plan. Weren't spontaneous decisions supposed to be exciting?

More like terrifying.

"Have you found Nicholas yet?" Avra asked, breaking her thoughts.

"No, I've been trying to find him. I'm exhausted. Honestly, I think I might just take off..."

"Babe, I looked him up and think you should stay."

Avra was bubbly and social and made friends quickly wherever she went. The concept of social anxiety was lost on her friend, and although Avra hadn't said it, it was clear she knew Miranda was nervous. Although Miranda was definitely the less social of the duo, they had been loyal friends since Miranda's last year of high school. Although Miranda had gone away to Ireland and Avra to Toronto, where she had later gone to law school, the two of them had moved back to Montreal around the same time. Their friendship had picked up right where it left off.

Come on, Miranda willed herself. *This is fun. This is going to be a great evening.*

"I'm going to grab some air," she said to Avra before saying goodbye and hanging up.

She couldn't help but wonder if coming tonight was a mistake. She didn't know anyone. Miranda made her way down the elegant staircase. All around her, people were clinking their glasses together and having what looked like the best time in the world. Through the large windows, the cool outdoors called to her. She had had enough of this party. Since being there, the sky had turned a rich shade of navy that glittered with stars.

Maybe Monaco is a mistake.

The thought struck her on her way out the door, as a man narrowly avoided spilling his glass of wine on her. Her dad, Chris, had loved parties like this. He had been the life of any party. Her other dad, Kyle, was an introvert, like her. She cast one last glance behind her at the party as she walked out the door. What did she think—coming back and believing she would fit in with her old world seamlessly? That she was going to feel any sort of connection to her dad by being here? She felt lonely and tired. She wanted to go home.

She made her way down the laneway and the road she had originally walked up. Now, it was filled with even more cars. She took a breath of fresh, salty air. Something about it, the familiar and comforting was the air wrapped around her, came up as a foggy haze of memory. Finally, something that felt consistent with how her dads described Monaco.

"...and you know how he will be this year..." The nearby voice of a woman penetrated Miranda's thoughts. "... he'll be more intense...harder on himself than he already is. I'm worried about him..."

A male voice murmured something back, but Miranda had difficulty hearing. Whatever it was, it sounded like an intimate conversation. Miranda did her best to avoid eye contact with the mysterious woman wherever they were. It was hard to make things out in the dark.

She made a sharp right when she got to the end of the driveway and made the mistake of looking back. Miranda saw the eyes of a woman who was grabbing something from a nearby car, the inside light now illuminated, appraising her.

She knows I'm listening. Come on, Miranda. Say something.

"Gorgeous night, isn't it?" she heard herself saying, wincing at hearing herself make the kind of small talk she had heard from her parents growing up and sworn she would never partake in.

Glancing up at the woman, who was now shutting the car door and walking towards her, Miranda felt the sudden impulse to leave. She didn't know why. She was nearly on the balls of her feet by the time the woman spoke.

"Miranda? Is that you?"

Like lightning, that voice struck a part of her memory she hadn't accessed in a decade. "Charlotte?"

Laughing, Charlotte's face became more evident in the moonlight, and it was the woman whom Miranda remembered so fondly. Suddenly, she was flooded with memories of her childhood spent at Charlotte and Freddie's apartment watching races on the television on Sunday morning with Nicholas, the two of them amicably arguing over who was the best driver on the grid. From behind her, the jovial and warm expression of Freddie Ridgeport came into view.

Miranda couldn't help but feel bowled over by joy as she gave them kisses on each cheek. "I'm sorry, I didn't mean to eavesdrop," she told them sincerely. "It's so good to see you both."

Charlotte appeared to cast a wary glance at Freddie.

"Welcome home," Freddie said warmly. "We heard you came back."

"Come say hello to Nicholas," Charlotte pressed. "I know he'll be thrilled to see you."

"Oh, no. I'm actually on my way out," Miranda protested. "But I promise to make plans another time—"

"Nonsense, it will only take a quick sec," Freddie said jovially. "Nicholas!" he bellowed.

Miranda was ushered back into the house, where the music seemed louder and conversations more animated. She watched from the doorway as Nicholas emerged from the second floor and made his way down the staircase. Her heart jumped, and the music faded into the background, everything but him falling out of focus.

"Nicholas, come join the party!" Charlotte exclaimed.

Somehow, he seemed different than when she'd seen him bundled up in a hat and sunglasses. He had looked almost hunted then. Now, he looked anything but. He smiled with easy confidence as he took a sweeping glance at the room, and Miranda felt her throat tighten. Perhaps she wasn't in such a hurry to leave after all.

Now the same age as her, Nicholas had grown into a *man*. Her memories of him were from a much more innocent time. He strode towards her with his head held high, an easy smile as if he wasn't bothered about a party this size. As if they happened all the same.

Perhaps they did, Miranda wondered.

Miranda could make out the faint outline of a muscular body beneath through his navy pants and crisp starched button-down. Wavy light brown hair and stubble that made her stomach flip flop, his sun-kissed skin conjuring images of lazy days on yachts and afternoons by the pool. He slightly resembled her memory of him if she squinted. And he was, without a doubt, the most handsome man in that room. The room was more than filled with them.

Miranda was blatantly gawking at him, she quickly realized, as Charlotte beamed at her son who approached them. Still standing with Freddie and Charlotte by the door, Miranda looked down, then up and then down again as he approached. The entire mood of the room seemed to have quieted as Nicholas was now on the main floor, and everyone's eyes flit in his direction.

He's coming over here. Look attractive, Miranda told herself. She jutted her hip in what she felt was an attractive, alluring pose.

Charlotte's eyes veered towards her. "My dear, are you all right? Your shoes aren't hurting you, are they?"

So much for that, Miranda thought as she shook her head politely at Charlotte and played it off as a stretch.

Nicholas was steps away. Confident and attractive, he gave his mother a peck on the cheek and his father a nod before he locked eyes with Miranda. "Nice to see you again," he said quickly.

She couldn't help but notice how his voice was smooth and warm like honey melted in the sun. The corners of his eyes crinkled as he smiled, dimples forming on his cheeks. Suddenly, being at this party didn't seem *quite* so intimidating.

Out of the corner of her eye, the flash of shiny hair momentarily distracted her. Swiveling around, she surveyed the woman

84

walking towards them, her hips sashaying side to side like a model on the catwalk. A thought hit Miranda. *Was that his new girlfriend?* There had to be a way to find out if he was single.

I'm done with men, she reminded herself. But her resolve felt less resolute than before.

Miranda summoned courage from deep within her, butterflies swirling around her stomach. "This is a really nice party. Are we celebrating anything in particular?"

"I'm not much one for celebrating myself," Nicholas replied, leaning in when he spoke so as not to shout over the music. "This was all my parents' doing."

"I'm really glad you invited me," Miranda said throatily before she could stop herself. As soon as they were out there, Miranda regretted her words, feeling uncool and overenthusiastic. That was the opposite of Monaco. But Nicholas appeared to take it in appreciatively.

"I'm really glad you came," he said slowly.

"I didn't exactly have other plans," she said, trying to make him laugh.

"Nicholas, Miranda, seeing you two after so long is nice." The words came out of the blue and made them both look away from each other. Markus appeared as if from thin air. She had seen him around the office a few times but this was her first time running into him outside the clinic.

He held out a hand to Nicholas. "Congrats on the seat, man. It's going to be a great season. You signed up for our clinic yet?"

Nicholas scowled at him. "No. I haven't."

"You don't see a sports doctor?" Miranda found herself asking.

He shrugged. "I see a bunch of professionals. I have my team assembled."

Markus threw his arm around Miranda and gave her shoulder a squeeze. "It's wild to think about how we'll be working together. Together again. Just like the old days, right?"

Miranda forced a smile. Her ex had always been a tad overenthusiastic, and it had tended to rub Nicholas the wrong way. It seemed that nothing had changed.

"We'll be working together at Monaco Rehabilitation. Exciting, no?" Markus told Nicholas.

She could tell Nicholas' mind was already elsewhere. Someone pulled for his attention, and he murmured his apologies as they pulled him into another conversation with someone apparently "dying" to meet him. Was she imagining it when his eyes had lingered on hers?

"So," Markus said, turning his full attention to her. "I've got great news. You'll never believe who we've gotten you for your client. I think Doctor Elbar already mentioned him to you."

"Who?"

"Serge Versuvio."

"Who is that?" she asked absently. She found herself looking around for Nicholas. Why had Markus barged into their conversation?

Markus' eyes widened, and he leaned in to whisper. "Nicholas' biggest rival this upcoming season."

TEN
Nicholas

Now

H e was huffing and puffing as he finished his run and slowed to a walk. He had to be in the best shape of his life for the upcoming season, and his new fitness routine involved running the hills and hidden roads of the small country.

Ow. Nicholas winced with each step. Hadn't pushing himself too hard always been his problem? Why hadn't he stopped after feeling like he'd tweaked his left ankle?

"Nicholas!"

The voice calling him was familiar. He turned around to see Serge Versuvio walking towards him. It looked like the other driver had just finished a run, too. But no huffing and puffing. And definitely no hint of injury.

Heat rose in Nicholas' chest and he shook his head with disbelief. After everything that Serge had done, the other driver had the audacity to say hello?

This was why he needed to keep pushing himself. To beat Serge. That driver was the worst kind of person. Deceitful. Hurtful. And all done with killer precision.

"I have nothing to say to you," Nicholas said as Serge neared, preparing to walk off.

"Wait, wait, wait," Serge said in his usual affable tone as if there was no bad blood between them. "I thought we'd cleared the air."

Nicholas laughed incredulously.

Serge raised his hands and eyebrows as if in surrender, acting so clueless that it almost made Nicholas second-guess himself. Had he forgiven the other driver and forgotten?

Unlikely.

"I didn't know you were in Monaco right now," Serge said.

Nicholas had a vortex of emotions swirling through him. "Where else would I be?" he fumed.

Serge had started as a driver in Formula One a year after him. In fact, Nicholas had taken it upon himself to mentor the younger driver. Since his own career had taken off in that first year, he thought he could afford to devote some time to other pursuits. As his own career began to decline and he scored fewer points, fewer podiums, and his confidence plummetted, Serge had been there for him—even as the other driver's career was soaring. There weren't too many opportunities to make friends in the sport. It was cut throat. Nicholas thought he'd finally found one.

Now he wished he'd never met the guy.

"I'm going," Nicholas said, turning to leave.

"I hoped I would run into you. I bought a place here," Serge said animatedly, catching up with Nicholas and matching his pace. The driver seemed eager to win back Nicholas' friendship.

Nicholas couldn't help but roll his eyes. If there was one thing he remembered about Serge, his old friend *hated* being disliked. The other driver considered himself the 'nice guy-type'.

He sure fooled me, Nicholas thought.

Serge continued. "My contract is up for renewal this year. It's risky to take on an apartment without certainty about next year. Who knows where I'll land. I think, though, that I have some options," Serge laughed.

Nicholas felt his insides clench. It felt like Serge was rubbing his nose in it. But his old friends tone was as it always had been—lighthearted and easy-going. That was typical. But Nicholas knew Serge well enough to know he had two sides—the most likable person one could meet in real life and a killer on the track.

And Serge had betrayed him. He had arrived at the hotel where Chantal was staying early one day to surprise her. At the time, he had been under the delusion that she loved him as much as he did for her. He walked into their bedroom and found the other driver and her together.

He had left the scene and Chantal had tried running after him, telling him how sorry she was. That was all she could say at the time—that she was sorry.

Nicholas got in touch with his lawyer and filed for divorce the next day without speaking to either party. She moved out that week while he was away racing. And he had just learned the two were now an item after meeting with Chantal in London. He didn't need to know any more than that. All of this was blow to his self-esteem when he felt like his identity was already on shaky ground.

And to top it off, she was pregnant. With Serge's baby. Before their divorce was even final.

If the press caught wind of this...

"Please don't speak with me on the track," Nicholas turned to Serge and spoke clearly. "We are not friends anymore."

Serge nodded, looking as if he finally got the message.

There was already enough pressure on Nicholas to do well this year without all of the drama from Chantal and Serge following him around. He just wanted to forget the whole thing ever happened. But that would be impossible. This was his comeback year. The year of Nicholas. His whole self was wrapped up in being a driver. He had felt lost and listless since being cut from his team. This was his chance for redemption.

Both Nicholas and Serge knew the unspoken truth. Nicholas *had* to perform well this upcoming year. His own contract was up for renewal. And the rumor around the grid was that Serge was vying for his seat on the team Nicholas had gotten signed to. He'd have to beat out Serge to keep his place on the track.

"Well, see you," Nicholas said tightly and turned to leave. As Nicholas stepped away, Serge began to say something in a tone Nicholas hadn't heard before. The other driver sounded almost... embarrassed?

"We...we are in love. I wouldn't have done that if I thought it was a fling. And I'm...sorry."

Nicholas was sick of people apologizing to him. Thank goodness Nicholas wasn't facing the other driver. His cheeks were burning. The feelings of shame, hot and horrid, came rushing back to him, just like when he'd first seen the two of them together. Imagining the two of them, sneaking around and falling in love behind his back was unbearable.

And he knew this was Serge trying to make things right. He knew that. But there was something about the whole situation that he didn't feel ready to forgive.

When Nicholas said nothing in reply, Serge looked at his feet. "Right. Well, I'll get going then."

Serge jogged off, and Nicholas felt more motivated to win than ever. And if he didn't win, all that mattered was that he beat Serge.

ELEVEN

Miranda

Ten years ago

M iranda walked along the port with her dad, Chris, by her side. The stands were nearly set up for the Monaco Grand Prix. The roads were blocked off, and people were setting up traffic cones.

"Who do you think will win this year?" she asked.

"Maybe...you?"

Chris laughed like it was the greatest joke he'd ever told. She'd done a few rounds of go-karting recently, and her dad seemed keen on helping her steer towards success. She liked racing, but she liked being in the classroom more. The thrill of learning the intricacies around how the heart pumped blood to the parts of the body that needed it was equal to the rush she got from racing.

She didn't share that part of herself with many people.

Her dad, Chris, got it. Knowing what a bookworm she was, he tried to ensure she had some balance in her life when he pushed her to do things like racing.

"I know you're going to be a superstar in whatever you choose to do," he had told her. "And it seems like that might be something academic. I just don't want you to graduate and feel like you had no fun along the way."

91

The thing was, she did have fun. School was fun for her. Outside the classroom, Nicholas was always the person she turned to. Wherever he was, the excitement seemed to follow. He brought out an adventurous quality in her. And somehow, she felt totally comfortable being herself around him. When he brought out that side of her she didn't often show to others, she never felt like she was pretending.

"I don't know, dad," Miranda said as they continued their walk. The two of them went for walks together a few times each week. "I think something in the sciences might be more my path."

Chris nodded, and he stopped briefly to wave hello at some people he knew in a café. "How do you feel about us leaving Monaco?" he asked, his tone light, but she could tell he was serious.

"You've asked me this a million times," she moaned.

"I know—I know," he countered. "I just want to make sure you're okay with it."

"I already said I was."

"Alright then."

"Don't you believe me?" she asked after a beat.

He sighed. "It's going to be a big change. I don't know. Maybe we should wait until you're finished school."

She stopped. "Look. You and Dad always tell me to go after my dreams. Right? And isn't this idea of us moving to Montreal a dream for you and your career? A new adventure? A big exciting opportunity for us all?"

"Yes," he agreed. "Yes, to all of those things."

"Plus, I'm kind of excited for a change," she admitted. She had imagined what her new life could be like. She enjoyed the idea of trying something new. Besides, the one person she would seriously miss was about to get famous and probably forget her anyway. It would be easier to move on from her crush on him by being on the other side of the world.

"Are you sure?" Chris asked.

"Yes," she said. "I'm sure."

She nodded, taking in the sights and sounds around here.

Monaco would be hard to leave. Impossible to forget. But she would be back. This would be a chance to live somewhere new. Before her inevitable return. After all, how could she leave this place for long?

TWELVE
Miranda

Now

O h no. Oh no no no no no.

That morning, Miranda looked at the pictures that Avra had texted her that morning about, urging her to peek at. Miranda scrolled through Instagram, looking at pictures that made her stomach churn. Her eyes were puffy and red. It was Connor. And another woman. And a *ring*.

How had her dream life gone to someone else? Someone who probably didn't even know Connor the way that she did? Did that woman know Connor hated romantic movies because he was too moved by them (rather than generally disliking them)? Did she know that Connor was so scared of his life passing him by that *he didn't even want to get married?* That, to him, marriage signified another milestone that passed in his life, edging him one step closer to *death?*

These had been his words, Miranda recalled. He had said them to her on numerous occasions.

How had this one person gotten the life with him that she had always wanted? That she thought she could convince him of? It seemed someone else was capable of what she wasn't.

Miranda tossed her phone across the bed as gold sunlight poured through the open window. She could hear smell the salty air from the sea in the not-too-far-off distance. But she had had enough salt water to last her a lifetime that morning.

She wiped away another stray tear, determined it would be her last at least for that morning. Already, she had been texting Avra, but from the time difference, her best friend wouldn't be awake for hours.

Mentally, she replayed the conversation she had with Connor repeatedly. He *missed* her? Yeah, right. And just because she didn't want to get back together with him didn't mean she felt *nothing* for him. He had clearly proposed to this person some time between talking to her over the phone and that evening.

Clearly, he hadn't missed Miranda all that much.

She looked around her apartment, feeling in some ways like she couldn't return to Montreal anymore. Even though she was lonely here. Being lonely here was better than being miserable there.

After a croissant and two cups of coffee in bed, Miranda had willed herself into a better mood. Maybe her body was finally getting used to the new time zone. Although it was her day off that morning, she'd gotten up with her alarm and headed to the clinic to organize her office.

As she made her way back from the clinic to her apartment, she decided Monaco was even more beautiful than she'd remembered. She walked along a stunning road with iron lampposts and cream-colored stucco buildings on either side. When she'd grown up there, it had simply been her home—she hadn't thought much about it. Now, there was something quite thrilling about being back.

Her phone pinged and she checked the text from her dad, Kyle.

Have you gotten the car yet?

She let out an exhale.

Not yet she texted back, putting her phone in her purse.

Her dad, Kyle, had been asking her about the car. She still hadn't gotten around to taking a look at it yet. It was on her to-do list. But she didn't want to look at the car if she was honest with herself. Being in Monaco had felt a bit like a movie. Slightly unreal. A welcome distraction from all those feelings that were swirling around she'd had when she arrived. But it also brought back more memories than she had anticipated.

Seeing the car felt like the final step in accepting her dad was gone. And once that was done, what would be next? The car was a stark reminder that Chris wasn't here anymore and that she was in Monaco for more than a new life experience.

Maybe putting it off for another week wouldn't hurt.

"Miranda?"

She looked up, and coming out of the store was Nicholas. He held up his hand in a wave.

She broke into a grin. "Nicky! I thought you'd be at the first race already."

He walked towards her and shrugged. "I've still got time."

"You seem awfully relaxed for someone whose season starts in a few days."

His eyes burned into hers. "I'm confident."

She felt her heart pounding in her chest, and she looked away, her cheeks feeling flushed.

"So, how is the new job going?" he asked.

Miranda bit her lower lip. "It's going well," she said, unsure whether to tell him about working with his rival on the grid. Her mind flitted to the contract she'd signed. Absolutely no disclosure about the treatment he was receiving was to be conveyed to anyone within the racing world except for the driver's immediate team. It made sense. She understood it.

I wish I was working with Nicholas, she couldn't help but think.

"How's your training going?" she asked conversationally.

He looked a bit nervous. "It's going well," he said. He didn't give any more details. And she didn't want to pry.

"And how's everything else?" she asked, hoping to prolong their conversation.

He shifted from foot to foot. "I mean, pretty good."

"Good."

"Good."

Well, that seemed awkward. She took a deep breath. "Well, I guess I'll head off..."

"Nicholas?"

The two swiveled, and her eyes narrowed on a man snapping a photo of them with his phone. She looked back at Nicholas, who had a deep furrow in his brow.

"Nicky, are you okay?" she asked.

His cheeks were bright red, and he looked slightly queasy. "I'm—fine," he muttered. His eyes flitted to the man with his phone and flashed with anger.

"Nicholas! Nicholas Stefano!"

The man snapping the photos was getting nearer, and Nicholas forced a big grin.

"Hi there," Nicholas replied.

"Nicholas! Wow. It's you. Can I get an autograph? Rough year for you, with your divorce. Hopefully you have better luck on the track than the last time around," the fan said, shaking his head.

Nicholas smiled with ease, and only because Miranda knew him so well did she see his hands trembling as he signed the man's cap.

"Always nice to meet a fan," he said cordially before turning to Miranda.

"Let's get out of here," she said gently, touching his shoulder.

He turned to her and nodded. "Okay."

***

"Where are we?" Nicholas asked.

She was standing in the garage she'd been avoiding. In front of them was the iconic vintage car her dad had loved. They'd taken off the car cover. It had been the one she and Nicholas had driven in once before she left. Seeing it brought back a flurry of memories.

"Miranda?"

She turned to him, misty-eyed. "Yes. Sorry, I'm just a little lost in memories. This was my dad's car."

"Oh?"

97

She stepped towards it and touched the glossy exterior with one hand. After all this time, it was still in pristine condition.

"It's the reason I came back," she admitted.

"You came back for a car?" he asked sceptically.

She blinked back tears. "He left it to me in his will. I guess it was the one thing he didn't want to sell. Or transport. A part of him that was left behind in Monaco. I didn't even know about it until he...died."

When she usually talked about her dad's death, the words felt hollow. Not today. She wiped a tear from her cheek, annoyed with herself for not having anticipated this response. What was she thinking bringing Nicholas here?

Nicholas took a step towards her. "You don't talk about him much. His death."

She crossed her arms, wishing they could change the topic. "Yeah."

"Why did you bring me here?" he asked in a low voice.

She frowned, wishing she had a good answer for him. "I guess it's the only private place in Monaco I know. At least, anymore."

"You wanted to go somewhere private?" he asked.

"I got the feeling you were a bit overwhelmed with the photo incident. And the stuff about your personal life being made public," she said quickly, averting her eyes from the car and looking at a cement wall instead.

He nodded. "Yeah. I—I've been having a more challenging time with that stuff."

She turned to him. "What stuff?"

"Fame."

He was looking at her and there was no way he hadn't noticed the few tears she couldn't seem to hold back. She was grateful that he didn't comment on it.

"Since we're sharing things," she began cautiously. "I don't think I'm doing this whole grief thing very well. I feel... numb. Most of the time."

Nicholas nodded, his eyes locked on hers.

"I'm just getting out of a relationship," she continued. Her words poured out of her and she wondered if she should stop. "It's been a nightmare year. First my dad, then my ex... and what's weird is that I have an easier time focusing on the breakup side of things. It's like my brain won't let me fully process the death yet. I've kept myself so busy within the last year. I took two weeks off after he died. And then a few months after going back, my ex asked me to move out, and then I had to keep working with him..." She wiped away a tear. "I'm sorry," she apologized with a laugh. "I've kept myself so busy these past few months. A lot is coming up."

"No need to say sorry." He took a step towards her. "You've had a hard year."

She nodded, this time without tears. In fact, she felt lighter than she had in a long time.

She forced herself to turn towards the car and took a step towards it, carefully opening the driver's seat door.

"Remember when we got stuck?" she began. Old leather and the smell of something sweet hit her nose. "Come on. Get in!" she said, climbing into the driver's seat.

The leather seats were smooth and shiny from years of use. Her dad had treasured the car but hardly treated it as precious. She could almost hear him saying: "What's the use in having something you love if you don't enjoy it?"

"I don't think we ever got stuck," Nicholas said, opening the passenger's side door and sitting beside her. The door shut with a heavy thud.

Miranda laughed. "You refused to admit it, even then."

Nicholas adjusted the seat and leaned back. "Do you think back about those days?"

"Sometimes." A small smile formed in the corners of her mouth.

"I remember everything," Nicholas admitted.

She felt a pang in her chest and she frowned. "Everything?"

"Back then, everything was simple," he said plainly.

"It wasn't simple!" she countered.

"No fame, no pressure...all the things I was working towards were things that would happen one day a long way off."

"And now?" she asked. She felt her pulse through her whole body. Everything around them was silent except for the gentle sound of their breath and words.

"I feel like I didn't live up to the vision I had for myself," he admitted. "Now I have a second chance to redeem myself. It's a lot of pressure."

"Haven't your dreams changed?"

He looked at her appraisingly and changed the topic after a beat. "How does it feel being back in the car?"

"Weird," she said truthfully, looking around as if a trinket of her father's might pop out at any second.

"It's in impeccable condition, especially considering the way we treated it," he said.

She looked around and had to agree. It was immaculately clean but visibly showed the years of happy memories. From the corner of her eye, she saw the thin stripe of pink nail polish from when she had painted her nails in the backseat. No one knew about that little accident except for her.

"Do you want to talk about him?" he asked her.

A lump formed in her throat, and she shook her head. "No," she managed. "I think I've done enough talking about it for today."

"Got it. So something lighter then. How was the breakup?" he teased.

She laughed. "I'm a mess. Can't you see?"

"You seem great to me. And how about...us?"

Her heart skipped a beat. "Us?" She turned to face him and immediately felt like a teenage again. Unable to tear their eyes from each other. That old car. Sneaking around.

"We're both fresh out of relationships," he said. "We could...enjoy spending time together. Without any pressure," he added quickly.

Instant butterflies. "I'd like that," she said.

"I'm sure you're not ready for anything serious," he managed.

"No," she agreed. "Things with me are...complicated."

"Complicated," he nodded. "That's exactly what things are like for me."

Tension blanketed them like a thick fog, the way it had all those years ago. She wanted to kiss him.

"So, you're not interested in a relationship," she started, feeling a small ripple of courage.

He didn't reply and just continued staring into her soul.

"I don't even know if I'm going to stay in Monaco," she admitted.

"Oh." He sounded a little bit sad and she couldn't help but feel pleased at this observation.

"But are you possibly interested in a...distraction?" she asked.

He slowly smiled. "Are you the distraction?"

She felt raw, sharing a part of her that she hadn't allowed herself to share with anyone else. Without thinking, she reached out to feel his cheek. It had stubble now. She thought she should have felt a mixture of emotions but felt calm. Instinctively, she leaned towards and placed her lips on his cheek, like it was the most natural thing in the world.

As she pulled away, his eyes met hers.

"Sorry," she muttered. "I don't know what got into me."

He shook his head. "No—don't be sorry."

Slowly, he leaned towards her, as if they were in a dance. She leaned to meet his lips. Without thinking, without worrying, without planning—she kissed him again.

THIRTEEN

Nicholas

Ten years ago

"Is it true?" Nicholas asked.

He was standing in Miranda's dads' living room. He'd heard the news from some people from his school that Miranda and her dads were moving. She hadn't been around that day—she had told him the day before that she would be in Nice to go shopping. But she hadn't mentioned the move to him directly.

He'd panicked when he heard and shrugged it off as a rumor. But when a second person asked him about it, he went straight to her house. Who knew when she would be getting home that day? He couldn't wait.

"Is what true?" Chris asked.

Kyle brought Nicholas a glass of sparkling water and sat across from him with Chris.

"You're moving. The rumor is going around."

"Oh dear." Chris looked at Kyle, who pulled a sympathetic face. "I may have let it slip to a friend last week. His daughter goes to school with them."

"Oh?" Kyle replied.

Chris ruefully shook his head. "I suppose we ought to tell him."

"Tell me what?" Nicholas asked.

Kyle sighed and looked at Nicholas kindly. "Yes. We're

moving."

"This is going to be hard for him," Chris said to Kyle as if Nicholas weren't sitting there. "The poor boy is in love with her."

Nicholas felt all kinds of emotions. They were moving? And *in love*? There was no way to either of those things. Was there?

"Where?" he demanded, his voice a few octaves higher than usual.

"Canada."

"Canada?" he echoed incredulously.

"Montreal, to be more specific."

His head was spinning. "But why?"

"Oh," Chris said, walking around the coffee table and sitting beside him. "I knew this would be difficult."

"Miranda should be here," Kyle agreed.

"Why?" he asked again. "Why are you leaving?"

"Because..." Kyle began.

Chris jumped in. "It's my fault," he said. "I went ahead and got a job as an art director of an incredible gallery. My dream job."

"It's an opportunity for something new," agreed Kyle. "We love it here. But we want Miranda to see that the world is larger than Monaco."

"If not now, when?" Chris said.

Nicholas scowled. "But why leave Monaco? Why not just go on vacation?"

"Maybe we'll be back in a year or two. Who knows," Chris said quietly. "But we might stay. We'll never know unless we try."

He folded his arms. "Is it wrong that I hope you guys hate it there?" he said, only half-kidding.

Kyle laughed lightly. "We know this will be hard for you. Given you and Miranda..."

"We're just friends," Nicholas corrected him automatically. He was used to people making assumptions about them.

Chris and Kyle looked at one another.

"Why don't you come visit?" Chris offered. "See a part of the world you've never been to?"

"Maybe," he agreed.

"Look, we know you are crazy for her," Kyle continued. "Why not tell her before we go?"

Nicholas was about to protest it, but from the looks on their faces, they wouldn't believe him anyway.

"And say what?" he asked with more edge than he meant.

"Whatever is in your heart," Chris told him. "And you never know. Maybe she feels the same way."

FOURTEEN
Miranda

Now

S he'd woken up with a mixture of embarrassment and elation. She'd kissed Nicholas!
If only her younger self could see her now. *I would be so embarrassed*, she told herself. *A distraction?*

She woke up in her own bed and opened the curtains, with golden sunlight pouring through. To her surprise, things felt a little better. After saying goodnight to Nicholas, she'd spent some time thinking about her dad. And why she was there. She hadn't gotten very far but she couldn't help but think it was a start.

As she made herself coffee, she felt a spark of hope. Things still felt like there was a lot of work to do—from her dad to Connor to everything in between. Her life had imploded so recently. She was just starting to rebuild it. And there was a seed of doubt in her mind about how realistic this was. Nicholas was about to have a hectic year with practically zero free time. She was about to do the same. Could they make something work?

Here you are, getting ahead of yourself.

She took her mug and brought it on her little balcony where she sipped her coffee in the sunshine. Miranda had the bad habit of imagining the future with practically everything. If this turned into a relationship, how would it work? And if it didn't? She felt almost nauseated at the thought of going through more heartbreak. Things felt delicate after her experience with Connor. And she was just scratching the surface about her dad. A part of her wondered if processing it all needed more attention.

Her phone buzzed and she thought it might be Nicholas. Shielding her eyes from the sun, she unlocked her phone. It was Connor. Her heart sank.

We need to talk. Are you free??? – the message read.

Another message popped up. *I might have made a mistake with us.*

She felt frozen. These were the words she had once desperately wanted to hear. A week earlier, it might have made a difference. But today, she felt more solid. More sure of herself.

She put her phone down and took another sip of coffee. And she didn't reply back.

***

There was a physician at the clinic that Doctor Elbar wanted her to meet. They weren't taking on new clients. According to Doctor Elbar, this physician was the best sports medicine specialist in the Riviera. And that was saying something.

Not long after Miranda had arrived at the clinic, the door to Doctor Inga Ivanov's room opened. Out walked a woman about ten years older than her, half of her hair shaved closed to her scalp, the rest bleached and cut bluntly into a bob. She wore a black shirt and beige leather pants that clung to her frame.

"You must be Miranda! Call me Inga," the doctor said, as her face burst into an electric smile. She walked towards Miranda with open arms. "You're just like your dad described," Inga continued as she drifted into the kitchen and put a coffee pod into the machine for herself.

She stood agog. "My dad?"

Inga smiled in her direction. "Chris? We went way back."

She shook her head. "You knew my dad, Chris?"

106

Inga nodded her head, and a look of concern crossed her face. "It was a while ago. Maybe just over a year when we last chatted? Back when you all lived in Monaco, your dad and I played tennis from time to time."

Miranda didn't know what to say. Did Inga know that he had...died? It wasn't exactly the sort of thing she wanted to discuss. And Miranda wondered what on Earth her dad had said.

Inga made her way from the kitchen and sat cross-legged on the floor in the small staff room in front of the glass coffee table, coffee cup in hand, all the while beaming up at her. "So, how are you liking Monaco?"

Miranda shifted uncomfortably. "It's beautiful. I always thought I would come back."

Inga smiled. "Your dad had mentioned you might return at some point in the future."

Miranda cocked her head to one side. "Really?"

The doctor nodded. "He didn't know when. But when I asked if you guys had plans to come back, he mentioned it might be in the cards for you. Anyways, I had reached out to him because I had a conference in Montreal. Come to think of it, he never did get back to me with a date. Montreal is great though. It's a beautiful city you guys moved to."

Miranda frowned. "You don't know, do you?"

"Know what?"

Miranda took a deep breath. She swallowed the lump in her throat. She could handle this. "My dad died a year ago." She let the emotions rise and fall like a wave within her. Another deep breath— she could handle this.

"I—I had no idea," Inga frowned. "I'm so sorry. What happened?"

"Heart attack," she replied. And she didn't feel numb while saying it. In fact, she felt like her heart was about to explode herself. She took a deep, steadying breath before the emotion passed.

"Wow," the doctor breathed. "I am so sorry."

She was used to people's condolences and people treating her like she was about to break at any moment. But Inga's tone felt different. Sincere but not assuming that she was crumbling. Maybe she wasn't.

"It's funny that my dad mentioned I might move back. I came here on a bit of an impulse. It felt like a good idea to get away," Miranda opened up, avoiding Inga's inquisitive gaze as she felt slightly uncomfortable opening up to a stranger. Words began to tumble from her mouth before she could stop herself. "I just got out of a relationship. And things in my life were...messy when I left. Really, it's so unlike me to have taken the job."

"Are you still feeling lost?" Inga asked.

"A little less so," she replied truthfully. "It's hard being away from my other dad, Kyle. I'm not sure if you knew him."

Inga shook her head.

"And being away from my best friend is hard, too. It's amazing being here," she confided. "But it's bringing up a lot too."

"Here, I'll grab your coffee. Not that I normally make a habit of it," Inga said, eyeing Miranda as if she might try to make it happen every day at work. "But in this case..."

Miranda smiled, feeling just a tad better than she had earlier. Inga was quirky and kind, she decided. "Thanks."

"Well, if you're in need of company, Monaco is full of the worst kind of men you can imagine. Rich, handsome, and some of them even interesting," Inga said, gesturing, sticking her finger down her throat as if to vomit. "The absolute worst," she teased with a glint in her eye.

Miranda couldn't help but laugh.

"And your ex? Are you over him?"

"I don't know," she told Inga. "It might take some time. I've kept myself so distracted over the last year, I don't know if I've really let myself process anything. And I'm worried that I'll keep overscheduling myself, giving myself more distractions..."

"It sounds like you need some time by yourself. To heal. To

process things."

Miranda nodded. "Are you sure you're not a therapist, too?" she asked with a laugh.

Inga smiled. "It's important to have colleagues you can lean on. Especially as the two women in the office."

"Yeah," she said, this time with certainty. "I think you're right. About all of that."

"Good. Because I have a lot of wisdom to share with you," Inga said in a teasing tone. "But seriously, if you're looking for interesting clients, this is the place."

Miranda smiled and looked around. This beautiful clinic. People now urging her to stay. When was the last time she had said *yes* to herself? Even Monaco had been more an act of desperation. Something to escape to.

Miranda felt herself nodding before the words even escaped her lips. "You know what? I cannot wait."

***

She felt like she was seeing everything for the first time. As Miranda walked to her office that morning, she was perhaps in the prettiest place on Earth. How had she not realized? The hazy golden sunlight bounced off the wrought iron balconies. The putty-colored buildings had gelato-colored flowers spilling off of them. Smatterings of French, Italian, and languages she didn't understand were spoken by people who passed by. Was this *really* her home? Her memories were hardly as glamorous—it had been normal when she grew up there. How her perspective had changed.

Stepping into the cool, modern lobby of Monaco Rehab, she felt almost self-conscious. Everyone was so...what was the word? Poised? This was much more impressive than the dinky clinic she was used to with... *him* working there, too. She reckoned that, at this point, he didn't even deserve to be named in her mind.

Since making her decision earlier that day, she had sent him one final text message at Inga's urging. She felt almost drunk as she peered at the words on her screen, barely believing she dared to send it. The

109

briefest of panics had begun to come over her now that she had. She blinked once again as she stared at the words she had typed out.

See you never. I'm staying in Monaco.

She frowned. Somehow, it seemed less cool than when she had sent it.

A knocking sound at her office door brought her back to the present. Her very first client of the day. As she had seen in her calendar, Serge—the racecar driver—had asked her to work with him one-on-one the day before.

"Let's see if you can help me," Serge began, sitting opposite her. "Now the work really begins. I have some fierce competition this year."

Miranda got to work with him, asking questions to get to know him better.

Serge grinned. "I like defying the expectations that people have of me."

She smiled and made a note. "And what expectations are those?"

Serge looked thoughtful but ignored the question. "And have you put any more thought into my offer?"

Miranda briefly paused. In fact, she hadn't. She thought about Nicholas.

But what did she have to lose? She wracked her mind, trying to devise a reason not to. Nicholas. Her heart sank into her stomach. But the two of them weren't in a relationship. They weren't exclusive. She had to do what was best for her and her career. Of course, she wouldn't do it behind Nicholas' back—that would be a conversation she wasn't looking forward to.

She took a deep breath. "Why not," she heard herself saying. "Let me talk it over with the clinic director. But—but for now, yes. A tentative yes."

***

The next few days passed quickly and the clinic was bustling. Every room in the facility was booked. Famous and familiar-looking faces had been in and out of the waiting room all morning. *Discretion* was the motto of the facility. She'd been so busy, she hadn't had much time to think about anything other than work.

"You can't get excited to meet anyone notable," Markus had insisted that morning. "They are here for treatment. Not to meet a fan."

Truthfully, she'd been so enmeshed with her schoolwork over the last few years that she'd barely had time to keep up with celebrity and sports gossip. If she recognized a famous face, it was because they were so obviously a household name that it would have been harder *not* to know of them. So far, she was mid-way through her day and had worked with a runner who had fractured her ankle, a former tennis pro working on their shoulder mobility. Now, she was waiting for Serge to arrive.

The room she worked out of was small but well-equipped. She would meet with the client in each appointment to discuss their progress, pain, and goals. Then, she would take them through daily exercises to help them. The facility was equipped with a gym for the clients to work on activities that clinicians recommended. Today, she expected to continue helping Serge with his tibialis posterior tendon using the resistance band, step-downs, and heel raises.

"Knock knock?" Markus peeked his head into her office. "How's everything coming along?"

She looked up from her notes. "Fine, thanks," she replied truthfully.

He looked like he wanted to talk. "And...and your day has been good?"

She smiled and shut her laptop. "Yes."

He looked relieved. "Good."

"Is everything okay?" she asked.

Markus took a step into the office. "I'm glad you asked. I wanted to see how you're enjoying being back."

"Honestly?"

He nodded.

"It's been such a blur. I dove into work almost the second I arrived. But I've enjoyed it," she said truthfully.

"Brilliant," Markus said. "What are your plans for this weekend?"

She thought back to her packed schedule. "Working."

"I really shouldn't say anything," he whispered. "But if things go well with your contract, a full-time position might open up at the end of the year."

Her eyes widened. "Hmm. Interesting."

He nodded. "Just think. If everything goes well, you could stay."

She wasn't sure how she felt about that scenario. "Right," she finally managed. "I'd better get back to my notes," she said, pulling a face. Serge would be there any minute, and she liked to be prepared.

"He's here!" Markus said, ushering in the driver. "Serge. Nice to see you! How are you feeling?"

"All right," Serge replied coolly. "A bit better with treatment."

"Good, good," Markus said amiably. "That's what I like to hear. I'll leave you to it."

"It sounds like you're feeling well," she began. "Let's see how your calf is doing today."

"I need to ask you a question first," Serge said, barrelling past her and taking a seat. "You know that I am in major competition this year. It is potentially the biggest year of my career. I need to beat Nicholas. You know his reputation. Everyone either has him pegged as my number-one competition for the upcoming season...or he'll be a flop. I could be a world champion. We need to make this happen."

"Right," she breathed. Nicholas. She felt a shiver run down her spine at his mere mention. And they hadn't seen each other since their kiss. He had messaged her, asking if she was free, but her work schedule had been more hectic than she'd anticipated. She got a swooping feeling thinking about him.

"I need you to help me beat him," he said. "How can we do that?"

"Serge," she began. Her client didn't need to know everything, but at the very least, she needed to see that she was....*something* with Nicholas. "I think you need to know—"

"—I mean, winning the world champion is just...I can almost feel it," he said animatedly.

"Right. Well, the thing is—"

"—Don't you think I can beat him?" Serge interrupted.

"Knock knock?"

Miranda looked up to see Markus at the door.

"Serge? Could I see you for a quick second?" Markus asked.

Serge nodded and walked out of the room to meet Markus. She heard them chatting in the hall before Markus returned alone.

"What's up?" Miranda asked.

"Serge left his cell phone in the lobby, and I once got in trouble with him for touching it when he left it in our gym in the past. So I let him know that no one has touched the phone and it's on the yoga matt," he said, mock rolling his eyes. "I'll be sure to never make *that* mistake again."

Miranda wrinkled her nose. "Got it," she said. Some of these clients could be particular.

Markus' eyes softened. "I read something that you might want to see, by the way."

He handed her his phone, which included candid-looking photos of Nicholas. And another woman. Adjacent was the headline: "Nicholas and his Wife—On The Track to Recovery?" The subtext included information from "sources," citing that after a brief period of separation, the couple was willing to "work on the marriage" and that they were "stronger than ever".

Her heart sank. "Why are you showing *me*?"

Markus' eyes softened. "I thought there might have been something there. I got that vibe at his party. Anyways, just thought you might want to know."

She nodded. "Thanks."

He pulled a face. "Serge is on his way back. I've got to finish up with some billing stuff. Anyways, have a good session."

"Thanks," she muttered.

As Serge came back, he took a seat. "So, what was it I was saying?"

Miranda took a deep breath. She tuned out her emotions, which would undoubtedly well into tears if she indulged them. "You asked me if I could help you beat your competition."

Serge's face lit up. "That's right. So can you?"

She paused for a second. She had never thought of herself as vindictive. Maybe that headline had been wrong? "I just have to clear something up."

Serge shrugged. "All right."

Her eyes narrowed. "May I ask you something?"

"Go ahead."

"Why do you want to work with me? I mean, I'm new to the clinic. You don't know me very well," she laughed.

Serge hummed and hawed before answering. "You are hungry. You haven't quite made it yet. Am I right? You're still in the process of proving yourself, no? In my experience, the people on the cusp of success tend to work the hardest. I hope you'll prove me right."

Her eyes narrowed. "Interesting."

She didn't succumb to pressure quickly. "I need to clear something up. But I'll call you tomorrow to book our next appointment if I can help you."

Serge shrugged. "You will get my voicemail. But have Markus call my assistant," he said. "*À bientôt.*"

Miranda thought of the tradeoff. Help Nicholas' rival on the grid potentially get a permanent contract. And if Nicholas was back with his ex—his wife—well, that was another matter. They weren't an item anyway.

At the end of the day, she left the clinic clear about one thing: she needed some clarity.

FIFTEEN
Nicholas

Now

W hen he had gotten a text from Miranda asking to meet up, he had immediately replied and hopped in of the shower, thinking about how much things had changed for him in the last few months. And how much he couldn't tell Miranda.

He had already confided to her about his divorce. That hit the newsstands with a force that rocked him. Reporters had swarmed his apartment when the news broke, but the story had died. He was able to breathe again. Until the next big thing.

"I need to talk to you," Miranda said as soon as he opened the door.

"No problem." He opened the door, and she walked in, making herself comfortable on the chair across from the sofa.

"Wow. It hasn't changed at all," Miranda murmured as she looked around, touching one of the delicately framed photos on the wall.

"Yeah," he said quickly, sitting across from her and feeling suddenly self-conscious. "I've been meaning to do something about it."

She smiled and looked at him squarely. "So, I've got something to say."

He leaned forward. "Oh yeah?"

She nodded and began to fidget with her watch. "I've gotten a request to work with another driver."

"Oh?"

"And I wanted to know where we stood."

Nicholas slowly leaned back. His brow creased, and he felt a familiar pang in his chest. "Well, I mean, what do you want?"

She looked down. "I just read an interesting headline."

He shook his head. "It's not true. At all. There's not a chance we're getting back together."

She frowned but looked like she believed him. "All right. Well, I guess you don't really owe me anything," she said with a laugh. "But I guess I just...wanted to check."

"Makes sense."

She paused, looking uncertain. "You know, I think I need to take some time for...me. I know we said that we weren't ready for anything serious, but I don't think I'm ready for...*anything*. And I haven't really given myself a lot of time to process things this past year. Or heal. I'm kind of a mess," she admitted.

He was sad to hear that but knew she was right. "Yeah. The timing just isn't right. We're both coming out of relationships."

"Alright then. So that's that," she said crisply. A flash of emotion he couldn't place crossed her face. "Friends?"

He grinned. "Of course." He scanned her face for any sign that she knew what he was up against. "Can you tell me who you're working with?"

"I'd rather not say," she began. "You'll find out soon enough."

"So you're planning on being at the track?"

Her eyes narrowed. "Like I said, you'll find out soon enough."

Silence fell between them, and the whole world faded before he spoke again. "So I guess your goal is to help this other driver beat me?"

"I suppose so."

Nicholas cocked his head to the side. He hated whichever driver had somehow gotten Miranda sucked into his charades. Two could play at that game. "All is fair in love and racing, I suppose. It's game on," he said, hoping he sounded more enthusiastic than he felt.

Miranda slowly smiled. "All is fair in love and racing," she agreed. "Game on."

***

Memories of his conversation echoed in his head as music blasted in his headphones. He was sitting in his Formula One car, trying to drown out his thoughts and pump himself up. Miranda had asked him about his thoughts on her working with another Formula One driver. She hadn't specified *who*. His mind flitted to all the other drivers on the track. He had replied in what he thought was her best interest.

But he couldn't help feel a bit jealous.

Was it regret? They weren't an item. But there was definitely *something* there.

With his hands gripping the wheel and the engine's vibrations rumbling through his whole body, Nicholas gave his team the go-ahead. Off he sped for his first lap of pre-season testing. It was also his first lap since returning as a Formula One driver, with cameras and media around every corner. Every hair of his stood on edge as he powered through turns and accelerated through the straightaways. This felt familiar. A grin spread across his face. He had dreamt of this opportunity for much of the last few years.

The significance of the drive was more important than his emotions. Pre-season testing spanned three days before the races started for the year. It was a chance to test the car to its very limit. Every season, a new car was unveiled for the team. This was the first time all drivers were testing their vehicles. Sometimes, the car performed like a dream. Other times, pre-season testing clarified that the engineers and mechanical team had their work cut out. Today was not one of those days for Nicholas and his team. For the other teams, that was another story.

Usually, at ten o'clock, Nicholas was busy with his morning workout routine at his apartment in Monaco. Now, blistering rays of sun beat down on him. Sweat poured down his body. No muscle group worked in isolation on the track; every muscle in his body was fully contracted. His heart felt on the verge of explosion as it thumped in his chest. He made another turn.

Perfection, Nicholas thought. *My first time in a Formula One car in a long time and it already feels natural.*

This was what his dad had been telling him about—*assured* him. Nicholas had needed that extra bolstering of confidence before today. His father, Freddie, played many roles in his life, from confidant to manager. It helped that his old man was also a former Formula One driver and world champion himself.

"Nicholas, see if you can push the car a little sooner at the next corner," his unfailingly polite race engineer said over the radio.

Nicholas had to give his team credit. The moment he accelerated a second earlier than his instincts told him, the car sped into action. Getting to know a car was like starting a brand-new relationship. Right now, they were on a first date—it was going very well, much better than expected, but there was a lot to learn.

"All right, Nicholas, you can come in now. Good job. A great start," came his race engineers voice over the radio.

The car lurched forward as Nicholas decelerated to make the track exit. He was still getting used to the way it handled. Although there were still a few kinks to work out, Nicholas was beaming, his heart light, his cheeks flushed. He hadn't felt this way in years. This was about as good of a first start as he could have hoped.

And he couldn't help but feel this was the beginning of a passionate love affair. But he hoped he didn't crash and burn like things had gone with Chantal. He hadn't commented when reporters asked him about the divorce. Or the rumors. Frankly, he had nothing to say. He was keeping his head down and focusing on one thing.

To him, the sport was about learning a shared language with the vehicle. Understanding its likes and dislikes. Knowing how far he could push it before it failed. Maximizing the strengths. He had gotten lucky many times on the track throughout his racing career, feeling there were some cars he positively adored. But unfortunately, he had not had as much luck in love off the racing circuit.

Slowing the car and pulling into the paddock, where his team and mechanics were waiting, Nicholas was met with a roar of applause. This was the applause he had dreamt of to start the season. It was the dream beginning to his second chance.

He felt on top of the world. He looked around and as he did, he caught a glimpse of a familiar face. There was Miranda. Was he hallucinating how attractive she had become from adrenaline? Had the pressure he was under for the last ten years finally cracked him? She was walking with a team in bright yellow shirts. That only meant one thing.

He took a few deep breaths. Surely she wasn't working for who he thought she was.

I've got to say hello to her.

"Nicholas, what a race! No one expected this from you, no one," Freddie said, meeting him as he frantically took off his helmet to try and get a better look.

Nicholas' head swiveled to see where Miranda had gone, but disappeared. Maybe he was imagining things from the heat? Everyone had reminded him that Melbourne was a fantastic grid but warned him to drink more water than he thought he would need. He was dripping in sweat.

Definitely dehydration, Nicholas determined.

"The oldest driver on the track today, and it seems you're also one of the fastest," Freddie chortled. "I think my genes are kicking in."

Nicholas fought the urge to roll his eyes, his father's commentary pulling him from his blissed-out stupor. "Yes, not the hours of hard work I've put in since I was *nine*."

Freddie paused for a beat. "That too."

The paddock now had its two cars side-by-side. This year, they were navy blue with silver accents, oversized F's that stood for the team name, and many logos from corporate sponsors. Just like all of the ten teams in the sport, Nicholas' team had two drivers: himself and Stavros Bilos. Unlike him, Stavros' career had been hot since being signed a few years earlier. No hiatus for that young driver.

In fact, Stavros had almost won the world champion title the year before. Three years into the sport, his teammate had become known for his aggressive driving style and fearless approach. Fans loved him or hated him.

Since signing his contract for the Fairway team, Nicholas had tried to remain neutral with his opinion of his teammate. After all, this was an ample opportunity for him. Before they met, he was hopeful they might have a cordial relationship. Nicholas had some tolerable rapports with his teammates in the past. But so far, their working relationship would be professional at best.

Fairway was a newer racing team, having only been around for three years. Stavros was one of the two original drivers they had acquired. Nicholas was replacing a formidable and experienced driver who, over the last two seasons, simply couldn't handle the pressure of competing with Stavros. That was the sport.

"You're only as good as your last race," Freddie had often told Nicholas growing up.

And Nicholas had taken it to heart.

Fairway had made it clear to Nicholas that they needed someone consistent, determined, and reliable—someone who could always be counted on to be in the top five. And with the right car, they thought that could be Nicholas. The driver they axed had been great and occasionally won races, but there were other days where he fell into the lowest rankings. This year, Fairway was striving to be the number one team, which meant that both drivers needed to perform nearly perfectly in each race.

Plus, Nicholas was apparently a fan favorite. Bringing him out of retirement was good for him and the team's image.

"They made the right call going with a veteran driver," his father told him as he stepped out of the car, and the two of them walked toward his engineer to debrief.

"I made a good choice with you," Dylan Rampart said in his usual booming voice. "Wasn't he a good choice?"

Glowing at the praise, Nicholas thanked the CEO as he told him to "keep it up." Nicholas promised him he would. Being given a second chance for a world championship title was what he had wanted more than anything. Nicholas grinned and tried to keep his composure, crossing and uncrossing his arms compulsively. Why did he suddenly feel so frazzled?

Although the team was new to the sport, the CEO they had chosen to run it certainly wasn't. Dylan Rampart had spent a few years as a driver himself, and although respectable on track, the man had found his true calling behind the scenes. Dylan had taken a chance on him, a "seasoned driver with a legendary father and a reputation as being a fan favorite"—those had been Dylan's words, not his.

Once Dylan had disappeared in a throng of crewmembers and the crowd around them thinned out, Nicholas turned to his father. "Did I just see Miranda walking in our paddock? Or am I going nuts?" he asked his dad in hushed tones.

"No. I haven't seen her," Freddie replied.

Zooooooooooooooooooom.

Skyrocketing by everyone in the bright yellow beauty of an automobile was Serge, driving for Canary. Serge had come close to winning the last world championship after going head-to-head all season with Nicholas' new teammate, Stavros, before the two lost to a third driver who had retired on a high note. Unlike Stavros, Serge was generally considered in the sporting world to be a fair driver. The fans universally loved him.

Nicholas did not share that sentiment.

"If you perform as well this season as you did today, you will obliterate him," Freddie considered as the two of them assessed the drivers on the track, the same way they had together for a decade.

Nicholas held his helmet in front of him, imagining the impossible. An electric thrill ran through him.

"I'm going to speak with Dylan..." Freddie said, a determined look on his face. "...make sure that there's no favored driver this year."

His day was all work. Nicholas headed towards a complete debrief with his team, which included Stavros.

"I thought I saw you."

The voice came from behind him, sending chills up Nicholas' spine. It was unmistakable. Miranda. And she looked downright perfect.

Her piercing eyes made his already heated body flush from the very roots of his hair to his cheeks. Truthfully, he had pushed all thoughts other than the upcoming racing season from his mind. He had been busy getting ready for this moment.

Had he totally missed out?

"Look at you." She spoke in her usual unassuming manner, making him feel more relaxed and turbocharged. "Doing so well at your very first race. I can't say I'm surprised," she breathed, not once breaking eye contact.

Without meaning to, images of his happy future with her were already forming in his just-a-tad-too-idealistic mind. Finally, he had the career he had always dreamt of. Finally, everything was falling into place. Maybe he really could still have it all? To have Miranda by his side sure wouldn't hurt.

Nicholas could feel himself flushing. Thank goodness for the fact that it could be attributed to him just having raced. "Somehow, I managed to get here," Nicholas shrugged, hoping he came across as indifferent as he was trying to be. Truthfully, he wanted to fist-pump the air that she had witnessed his last lap.

He was reminded of those moments when he started racing. His obsession with racing was somewhat to get her attention in the first place. How could he forget? Miranda was his first crush. He bit back a smile, thinking about how convinced he was when he was young that she was his first love. Of course, she had never known that. She moved before he could ever proclaim it. But he had been a kid back then. It didn't mean anything.

"I don't think anyone is the least bit surprised with how things went today," Miranda continued with easy confidence and a laugh.

"So," he began, his heart pounding in his chest. "I saw you in a yellow shirt."

She nodded. "Yes. I'm working with a driver at Canary."

His eyes narrowed. "Not Serge?"

She shrugged. "I guess you'd find out soon enough. But yes, Serge."

A part of him felt like he was about to explode. Serge? *Serge*??? How had this driver managed to ruin his marriage and work with Miranda? Did Serge know what he was doing? Or was Serge utterly clueless, as he instinctively knew that the other driver could be?

More importantly, did Miranda know?

From the look on her face, she had no clue about how things had played out between him and his former friend.

"So, Serge?" he asked again, eyes like saucers.

"Yes," she replied in a straightforward tone.

His mind was reeling. Anger, hot and all consuming, raced through him. Should he tell her? Did he need to tell her? He felt too angry to speak. Too embarrassed to tell her the truth. And if he told her, and she continued working with the other driver, wouldn't that change things between them? Miranda looked serene. Not like someone who was trying to sabotage him. Her career was taking off. And she didn't owe him anything. Telling her would inevitably sour her professional relationship with the team. And he really didn't feel like talking about what happened. Eventually, the truth would have to come out.

But not today.

"I'd watch out for Serge if I were you," he finally said.

She offered a weak smile. "Okay."

She seemed to want to change the topic and frankly, so did he. It wasn't her fault that other drivers wanted to work with her. He couldn't blame her for that. But he could blame Serge.

"So you're here to cheer me on?" Nicholas prodded, feeling it was important to bring some lightness to their situation. He knew that she wasn't. But then again, there was no reason for her to be in his paddock. Wasn't she supposed to be with Serge?

Miranda pulled a face. "" Afraid not. I'm still here as a physician."

"And any chance you're looking for a new client?" he asked, only half-kidding.

Miranda laughed. "I'm afraid my signed contract is with Serge for the season."

"It looks like you've done a good job," Nicholas managed, his mind flitting to see how Serge flew around the track that day. It took every ounce of self-control not to smack talk his opponent. "And you just stopped by to say hello?" So what if Miranda wasn't in Australia to cheer him on for his first race? She was here in the paddock to see him now. She didn't have to do that.

"I'm just here to check out the opposition," she retorted.

Just seeing her there brought feelings back that he thought he'd gotten over. A small part of him still couldn't shake the hope that she was there to see him. Even for friends, it wasn't standard practice to walk into the paddock of other teams.

"I'm flattered you consider me competition. Just wait until I have a bit more time in the car. Serge won't see me coming."

"Probably because he'll be a half-lap ahead of you," Miranda teased.

"Where are you staying?" Nicholas asked, changing the subject as fast as his turns. Speaking with her now was just like old times. As the slight awkwardness of reuniting with his childhood friend wore off, he fell quickly into their old patterns of teasing and banter. It dawned on him how much he had missed it.

"The Harbour Inn. It's quaint."

"Dinner tonight?" asked Nicholas. As soon as the words were out, adrenaline flooded him like it had on the last turn.

Miranda's eyes narrowed as she appeared to weigh her options. "I'm working late, but if you can wait until eight-thirty, you're on."

"It's a date!" Nicholas beamed, immediately regretting how eager he sounded.

Miranda gave him a quizzical look before she said goodbye, giving off the air of someone unsure if they had just made the right decision.

**

Nicholas was done his first day on the grid, but things were just getting started. Instead of feeling tired, he felt revved up and fuelled with adrenaline. He knew he probably wouldn't sleep tonight from the elation of the day's events. And his anger towards Serge. He pushed that from his mind. The sun's warm glow lingered late into the early evening, spilling into his luxurious hotel suite, where he had flopped onto the bed as soon as the door closed. Down-filled and sweet smelling, Nicholas felt his muscles unclenching ever so slightly as he lay his head on the crisp white pillow.

Of all of the ways that today could have gone in his imagination, he never would have imagined it would go like it had today.

His hotel had been booked for him—this one, in particular, housed multiple drivers for the weekend. White leather and chrome chairs were arranged next to the floor-to-ceiling windows to maximize the view of the water. Small bouquets of white roses in white vases had been carefully placed around the room. It was the antidote to the chaos of the weeks leading up to this.

But even in such a serene setting, he still couldn't find it within himself to quiet his mind. His life was moving at a speed that rivaled his driving, and moments like this were becoming fewer and further between. He thought back to his driving and Miranda—nothing about the day felt real.

In the car, Nicholas was calm, confident, and self-assured. He privately struggled with anxiety outside the vehicle, although he never would have admitted it. He drummed his fingers on his nightstand and shifted restlessly on the bed. Only a few knew him well enough to guess what lay beneath those frenzied eyes. To him, driving was a domain he could control. There was an entire team to help him maximize his performance. He was on his own, out here in the world off the grid. He didn't quite know whether to trust his own instincts and choices.

Without driving to ground him over the last few years, his anxiety had been at an all-time high.

Pulling himself up with all the strength he could muster, he unpacked his neatly pressed shirts and carefully laid them onto the mussed bed. A team meeting over appetizers with the Dylan and his teammate, Stavros, was next on the itinerary. Nicholas looked at himself up and down in the mirror, changing into a linen button-down, beige slacks, leather slip-on loafers, and darkly tinted sunglasses for good measure.

"Confident, sexy, a winner," Nicholas told himself, trying to practice the positive self-talk that everyone spoke so highly of. "You can impress them—I mean, you're impressing them." His voice warbled slightly near the end.

What is going on with me? he thought.

There was one unifying trait of all the drivers on the grid—they all believed they were number one. It kept them all racing at those death-defying speeds week after week. Everyone thought they could beat the odds and win. They were the exception. Bad things wouldn't happen to them. They *couldn't*.

Nicholas knew that to win, he needed to cultivate that mindset. But somewhere deep within, he had a nagging fear plaguing him that he wouldn't be good enough. The fear had been creeping up ever since the contracts were signed.

What if he blew it? What if this second chance failed? He would never get another opportunity like this in a million years. It was now or never.

Nicholas took a deep breath, feeling the tension in his chest easing slightly.

He had worked hard for this. For some reason, the harder he tried to push the thoughts from his mind, the more often they popped up. Right now, he couldn't risk anything less than perfection. In fact, he couldn't risk anything less than perfection for the whole *year*.

Being in the presence of Stavros required steely resolve.

Impressing Dylan was paramount—and it had to be within the first few races. Especially if Serge was vying for his seat, as rumor had it. Dylan could start shopping for his replacement at any time. A one-year contract meant his seat the following season wasn't guaranteed. The races hadn't even started, and he was already thinking about his future. Everyone else on his team would be doing the same thing. He took a deep breath in and out, summoning the calm he yearned for. Surely, he could quell these feelings for a year.

Ten minutes later, he was the first to sit in the hotel restaurant, always having liked to be there before everyone else. He figured that it didn't hurt to give the impression of professionalism off the bat.

Dylan arrived second, wearing a button-up shirt tucked into neatly pressed pants. His slicked back, slightly thinning hair made him look more menacing than Nicholas knew him to be.

"What a start to the season. What a start," his boss greeted him warmly before clapping him on the back. "I knew with you. I told my guys that Nicholas is *our guy*."

Nicholas beamed. This wasn't the first time he was having his praises sung today. Everything seemed to be falling into place. So why did a knot seem to tighten in his chest?

"I'm grateful to be in this position today," he replied.

"Ah, there's our other star," Dylan said as Stavros approached.

Looking every bit the suave playboy that Stavros surely imagined himself to be, his teammate and main competition joined them. Stavros's printed shirt was likely from his latest collaboration with a major fashion house. Stavros flashed a slightly too charming grin towards Nicholas and their boss.

Nicholas forced back a taught smile. Growing up in Monaco, he had been given the rare opportunity to people-watch his entire life. He felt like he was pretty good at reading people. Stavros was *all* ego. And if there was one thing Nicholas had learned to handle after all his years of racing, it was managing people's egos.

"Old man, aren't you punching a bit above your weight with this car?" Stavros joked to Nicholas. He was the only one who laughed at his own joke.

Nicholas was only a few years older, but pointing that out wouldn't have done any good. "I think me and the car are getting along just fine," he retorted.

Stavros winked. "Ah, but only a master knows how to get everything possible from the machine. We will see if you are a master."

Nicholas chose to ignore his teammate, looking around the restaurant instead. The tables were sparse, and the chairs expensive-looking. The music played softly in the background, and the waiters wore black vests over white shirts. Dylan ordered sparkling water for the three of them and appetizers, and they got down to business.

"Today, we saw that our car performed exactly how we wanted it to," Dylan began. "We've got a great team this year, including the two of you. Our fan base is geared up. Stavros—you already have a following who think you could be a real contender for the world championship. Nicholas—you had a rough exit from the sport. But we're glad to see you back in. You've got personality and a legendary story behind you."

Dylan was referring to Nicholas' famous father; however, only a few people knew about his upbringing. The people who raised him until he was nine. The turmoil he endured before finding his biological parents. As someone who was naturally private, he was fighting hard to keep that information concealed beneath the hood. In fact, few people knew his story fully. When he thought about it, Miranda was one of the very few.

"This year," his boss continued. "I think we have a real chance of beating Serge and his team at Canary. They've narrowly beat us for the last two years in a row. Let's not let them have another. Stavros, we're going to be counting on you. You too, Nicholas," he added.

He bristled. Maybe he was being over-sensitive. But it seemed like no one expected him to be a leading contender to win the season. Although he and Stavros would be racing technically as a team, his teammate was coincidentally his most prominent competitor, given that

Stavros was the only other driver driving the exact same vehicle. How they performed on the grid would directly reflect their abilities. Nicholas was eager to prove himself. Who cared if he was obviously considered a secondary driver right now? He had time to prove himself.

"Nicholas, who was that girl I saw you chatting with? Punching again a bit above your weight once again, no?" Stavros prodded with a grin.

Nicholas smiled curtly. "Trust me, it doesn't concern you."

"This guy," Stavros continued, pointing at Nicholas. "Always wanting the best of everything. The best car, the pretty women..."

Nicholas wanted to retort that if he wanted the best of everything, he would be on a team that surely didn't have Stavros. Instead, he pursed his lips and looked away, embarrassed not by Stavros' words but by his antics. Heads were turning at other tables to look at them. Stavros was nonplused as he took a swig of his sparkling water.

Dylan, clearly adept at handling challenging personalities, swooped in. "We've got the best of it all this year. We really have a chance to win. I want us to maximize this potential. That means the two of you need to work as a team. I want photo ops, Instagram posts, and everything on social media you guys have going for you, cheering each other on and the team as a whole. Can you do that?"

Stavros sulked. Suddenly, he didn't have a snappy comeback. Nicholas thought this could be his opportunity to become mature and responsible, even though he would probably be mocked for it.

"You can count on me, Dylan." Truthfully, he had no idea how he would stomach posting a picture of him and Stavros being buddy-buddy together. He supposed if it were for his career, he would at least have to give it a shot. He looked at Stavros expectantly. Stavros glowered at him from across the table. Nicholas and Dylan continued talking, Stavros' silence notable as he appeared to be fuming at the idea of having to be friendly to his teammate. Things felt tense, awkward, and slightly embarrassing, like a collision at the race's first turn. If this was the trial run, things weren't off to a stellar start like he had hoped. Things would surely go better that evening.

***

"Wow, you're right on time," Miranda said, greeting him in the lobby of the inn she was staying at. "Nothing has changed."

Nicholas took her in, slightly breathless, from rushing from the team meeting to seeing her on time. Nothing had changed, and yet, everything between them had. She had evidently put in some effort for tonight's dinner with her wavy hair and intoxicating perfume. She wore a jumpsuit with sky-high heels, making Nicholas' heart pump incredibly fast in his chest.

Pace yourself, he told himself. *This is just the beginning lap. You have a long way to go.*

"How has everything been going at the clinic?" Nicholas asked as they walked to the restaurant where he had made them a reservation. He would tell her about Serge tonight. He didn't want to but it had to be done.

"I guess I've developed a reputation as an expert for high-performance athletes with neck injuries," Miranda laughed. "Apart from Serge, my first major client was a soccer player. Surprisingly, he had a weak neck. Well, he was not exactly weak, but he was definitely not strong enough to withstand the way he always took headers. He was about to get axed from the team before I met him. That, or he would have to leave the sport because his body just couldn't handle it anymore. But he recently scored a winning goal. Miraculously, it was a header that got the ball in."

"That's incredible," Nicholas replied.

"But it makes sense that a racecar driver would come to see me," Miranda continued. "You guys deal with such incredible G-forces. Your job is a lot more physically strenuous than most people think."

As Miranda spoke, memories he hadn't thought about in years about his childhood growing up with Miranda popped into his mind. She had always been a gifted athlete, putting him to shame when they jogged together up and down the craggy cliffs outside of Monaco.

130

Hadn't she won athlete of the year at their school? Unsurprisingly, she had leveraged her abilities to become who she was now. Clearly, she was passionate about what she did. His heart pounded as she spoke. She had always been confident, but now she radiated sureness that even some drivers lacked. Himself included.

"How are things with your dad back in Montreal?" he asked.

Her eyes dropped. It looked like she didn't want to talk about it. "Okay," she finally answered. "He's been having a hard time this last year."

He wrinkled his nose. He was no expert in grief, but he had lost his own adoptive parents when he was just a kid. If anyone knew how hard and complicated that process could be, he did. "It doesn't sound like it's been easy," he said.

"No. I think my dad has struggled more than he's willing to admit." She turned away with glassy eyes.

Time to change the subject.

"And how are things going with Serge?" he found himself asking.

Miranda smiled, her cheerful demeanor returning. "It's going really. And that's all the talk I will do with you about work."

His heart sunk. Things were going well with Serge. He really didn't want to burst her bubble. Especially on the heels of talking about her dad. "All right. Fine. So how about we talk about us."

"Us?" She sounded surprised. "I thought we'd figured that out."

"I mean our friendship," he quickly corrected himself. "I know things with us took a...turn."

She smiled. "Yes. The first time for us, which is a bit of a shock, come to think of it."

He thought about their kiss. "I had a crush on you way back then," he heard himself admitting.

Her cheeks flushed. "You did?"

Laughing, he nodded. "Big time. It was brutal when you left."

"I had a crush on you too!" she admitted.

His jaw dropped. "No. You're kidding!"

She shook her head. "I guess we never got the timing right, huh?"

The waiter arrived at their table and they ordered glasses of wine before he replied. "I guess not."

After a moment, Miranda looked up at him. "It was a good kiss though."

Nicholas laughed. "Yes. It was a good kiss."

"But definitely not the right timing," she added quickly.

"No. Definitely not," he agreed. He wished that it was. He wished it had been. But the two of them needed to work on themselves.

"Actually," Miranda began. "I feel like this takes a lot of pressure off the friendship. We've gotten the kiss out of the way."

"Right," he laughed. "Phew."

She laughed and took a sip of wine. He couldn't help but feel like there was still a spark there. Something between them.

"How are you doing with all of the changes?" he asked. "In all seriousness. I know you've been going through a lot."

"Good. Well, maybe not *good*. But better."

He nodded. "Me too."

She wrinkled her nose. "Honestly? I thought you were going to try to make something of tonight. To try something with me."

Nicholas took a deep breath. "Yeah, well, life might be easier if I tried, to be honest. It would mean that I was enjoying distractions in my life. And not trying to, you know, deal with things."

"I know what you mean," she said slowly. "I know what you mean."

He looked at her and took a deep breath. "So, you know, about this whole Serge thing—"

"—I want to thank you," she cut in. "For being so relaxed about it all. I mean, I know how competitive you guys are with each other," she laughed.

He took her in. All of her. From her smile to her eyes to the candlelit glow of her skin. The words were right there in his head. They just couldn't make their way to his lips.

"No problem," he heard himself saying instead. And as they sipped their wine and continue talking, Nicholas couldn't help but wonder if confessing the truth of how his marriage had ended was harder to admit to her or to himself.

***

He was back at the hotel and put down his phone. *What* did he just read? Another article about him and his wife getting back together? There was already that first headline. Now this? He hated to do it, but he had to call his ex. It was absurd to think she was still his wife.

"Chantal?"

He heard a few people in the background. "Nicholas?"

"Yes, it's me."

He heard the people in the background fade away as she presumably left for somewhere quieter.

"I didn't think I'd hear from you," she replied in a concerned tone. "You didn't return my calls."

He felt a little guilty about that. But then again, he also didn't feel like he owed her any more of his time. "We're supposed to go through the lawyers."

"So, why aren't you today?" she asked.

He took a deep breath, trying to keep his composure. "Have you read the article?"

The silence on the other end was telling. "A friend of mine sent it my way. I glanced at it."

"You glanced at it?" he echoed.

"Well, what do you expect me to do? I don't have any control over what people report. It's probably just click-bait."

He sighed, knowing she was probably right. "You're sure you don't know who sent these photos of us? They're old. I'm planning on having my lawyer reach out to them. Because I haven't seen you in ages."

"I don't appreciate what you're implying," she told him. "I didn't do anything shady here."

133

"Fine," he conceded. "I'll have my lawyers call yours to get this divorce finalized."

He said goodbye and hung up the phone, feeling more annoyed than he had in months. Right away, he had the urge to call Miranda.

Their dinner had ended on an amicable note and their conversation had steered towards racing, her career, and travel. When the night was over, she had given him a chaste peck on the cheek. Nothing too exciting. But he couldn't help but feel more excited by being with her, even as just friends, than he had felt in a long while.

SIXTEEN
Miranda

Now

T he foam on top of Miranda's cappuccino wobbled as she tried to control her trembling hands. Although she had heard the words, it felt incomprehensible that it was true.

"Serge is a great driver. An excellent driver. A potential world champion. Everyone expected him to do well this year, but not this well. He says that you are good at your job."

Griegor Velda, the team principal of Canary, had invited her for a six o'clock coffee, making her already jetlagged brain feel like it was working through a thick cloud of fog. When Griegor had begun singing her praises, the fog had vanished, leaving her feeling like she floated through a misty dream. Was this real?

"They say you bring athletes back from the dead," the boss continued with a smirk.

Miranda laughed. "I've brought a few athletes out of retirement. Sometimes away from the death of their careers. A requisite for all my clients is that they are living and breathing."

Griegor didn't laugh at her joke and surveyed her with a scrupulous expression on his face. "I'm looking for a physician who can work with not just one driver. A team player is harder to find than one would think. We need a new physician for the team. Ideally, it would be a permanent position. Does this...interest you?"

Miranda put down her drink with trembling hands, scared she would spill and embarrass herself in front of the man who seemed to be proposing a job.

A full-time job with a Formula One team? Miranda fought the urge to fist pump the air and instead took her time to respond, as Griegor seemed to choose his own words carefully.

The last few months in Monaco had gone surprisingly well. Miranda had gotten used to the rhythm of her new life. Her role as a doctor responsible for the driver's physical state went beyond just ensuring they were in peak physical shape; they were also trusted confidants, life coaches, and motivational speakers. She had a one-year contract at Monaco Rehab. And although Markus had brought up the possibility of a permanent position opening up, there was no guarantee for her future.

"The thing is," Griegor continued. "I haven't made up my mind about the idea. It all comes down to Serge's performance. Can he win a world championship with you, ensuring his body is in the best shape? It's fair to say our car isn't as competitive as it was last year. Still, he is doing a good job in it." Griegor's eyes narrowed. "Can you get him that win?"

Miranda gulped. She could read between the lines: if Serge won, she would have this job opportunity of a lifetime.

"I will do everything I can," she managed firmly. Her heart skipped a beat as they shook hands, unsure of what she was committing to but knowing that the ante had been upped.

"Just ensure that 'everything you can' is a podium in our driver's hand. Remember my favorite saying: First place is the only place."

First place is the only place? Miranda wanted to roll her eyes but kept walking past the makeshift offices each team had set up by the track. She loved the opportunities afforded to her. But she couldn't help but feel slightly put off. Her eyes kept darting from one person to the next, casually scanning faces. It might be nice to run into Nicholas, she thought.

"Nice job!" one of the team members called to her as she walked by.

She gave them a winning smile in return. Radiating sureness in her profession was one of Miranda's prized skills. She had a knack speaking with authority and commanding attention when it came to her patients.

Behind the facade, she was nervous. There had been a knot in her stomach since she'd landed. She had never worked with a Formula-One driver before, let alone for such an extended time or prestigious position, and she felt tremendous pressure not to screw it up. Her career was taking off much faster than her confidence. Somehow, enough people had believed she was capable of this. Was she? And was this what she wanted?

"We need to meet in ten minutes sharp." Serge's voice broke through her cluttered thoughts, making her jump. He was walking towards her with a sports drink in hand and an assistant walking a few steps behind him, who was muttering something into an earpiece.

"Same place as earlier?" Miranda asked.

Serge nodded before talking off towards the office with the assistant. So far, he was a good client and put in the work. From everything she knew, he seemed fully confident with her abilities, too.

She reached into her cross-body bag for her phone, eager to tell her father the possible good news. On second thought, she put her phone away. She didn't need to get his hopes up. Besides, she needed to meet Serge at the gym, she thought as she checked her watch.

The team's office was minimalist and luxurious. Nothing about it looked like it would be torn down and set up again halfway across the world within a few days. Since they were constantly moving and workouts were done on the road, she had invested in a percussive therapy massager to help Serge's recuperation after races. She fished it out from the bottom of her bag. The exercise instrument had cost her hundreds of dollars, but if she thought it would help, it was always worth the money.

"Okay! Let's see how you're doing today," Miranda asked

enthusiastically as she entered the clinic—although it didn't look like the clinics she was used to with its pale grey foam mats and large mirrors. She had found that if her energy was high, it increased the energy of the people around her.

Serge nodded from the floor and was already into some quad stretches. "I think I've got more competition this year than last."

"Oh yeah?" she said, putting her bag down and walking to the mat adjacent to him. "Who are you worried about?"

"Nicholas Stefano. Did you see his lap? I think he'll be strong." He listed a few more drivers before adding: "And that Stavros character. What do you think of him?"

"Dangerous," Miranda guessed. "Stavros is a liability. Albeit, a liability who might get his team podiums at the risk of other drivers' safety."

Serge nodded. "I think so too. So, you know any of these guys from your training?"

Miranda felt her breath catch in her throat. "I, uh, I know Nicholas from ages ago."

The driver frowned. "You *knew* him or you *know* him?"

Her stomach clenched into knots. Was this a deal breaker? "Both. We used to be friends. And we've run into each other since I got back to Monaco."

Serge stared at her with an unreadable expression. "Interesting. And, how does he feel about you working with me?"

She took a deep breath, evading the question. "This is my work. His opinion of what I do doesn't matter in this area of my life."

"True," Serge replied, continuing to survey her. "So you know that Nicholas and I..." he trailed off.

"What?" she asked.

His expression relaxed the more perplexed she felt. Did he know something she didn't? "It's nothing," he said lightly. "We used to be friends. That's all."

"Oh. He didn't mention that," she said, wondering what happened. She figured it would be hard to maintain friendships in this field.

Miranda tried to change the subject. "So, today, let's focus on your training and what you're going to do to set yourself apart."

This momentarily appeased Serge as he followed Miranda through a series of warm-ups. She moved on to the next exercise with Serge, finding herself of two minds. She wanted her childhood best friend and whatever their relationship had turned into to thrive; at the same time, she felt a spark igniting within her as she did her work. Good things would happen at her current job at Monaco Rehab and a potential position might even open up on this team if Serge won. She had these two exciting opportunities in front of her. She appraised Serge as he continued with the exercises she told him to do. He was a hard worker. And although his demeanor could be a bit curt, he seemed nice.

May the best racer win, she thought. Because in that moment, she decided she was going to give it her all.

***

She was catching up with Avra at the end of the day from her hotel room. The two of them hadn't had a proper catch-up since the Ridgeport's party. Her friend was perplexed as to why she and Nicholas weren't trying to make something work.

"Why?" Avra begged her to know over the phone. "I need a reason."

"Because," Miranda insisted. "I need to focus on me. I just got out of something. And so did he. I'm giving myself time to heal. Plus, if I gave it a shot with him, I would be saying no to a major career opportunity." It simply wasn't possible for things to work out between them if they were actively competing against each other. It would never work. The rational side of her mind focused on the work part and the emotional side of her focused on the healing part. Either way, she couldn't entertain things with Nicholas.

"Besides," she added. "He's not even legally divorced yet."

"If you say so," Avra said, her disdain audible. "I still think you should give him another chance."

"That race is long done," Miranda said. If she was being honest with herself, she knew that there was more to this than she was admitting. "I'm going to head to bed," she told her friend, stifling a yawn.

"Miranda? Before you go, I wanted to check in with you. How are you doing?"

"Fine," she replied stiffly. Of course, she was fine. She'd been fine this whole time.

Her friend appeared to know her well. "And how are things about being back...are you thinking about your dad?"

"Yes," she said, rubbing the crease between her brows. She really didn't want to get into this.

"If you say so. But I would be surprised if grieving didn't take longer than you think. It's not just...done."

"Yeah, well, I'm fine," she said. She didn't want to talk about it anymore. "I'll call you next week," she added, this time more softly.

Her friend agreed, and Miranda hung up. Her gut instinct had been right. She figured she needed to focus on herself. No distractions. No masking the pain.

Avra's words echoed in her mind. And it was fitting timing, because earlier that day she found out that she had a visitor coming. And she anticipated it would bring up more than she was prepared for.

She put her head on her pillow and willed herself to sleep. She could deal with reality later. Now, she just wanted to rest.

SEVENTEEN
Nicholas

Now

" All is fair in war, right?" Nicholas laughed, doing his final run down with his team before the season's first race. "We'll do everything we have to do to win. But we'll also expect every other team to do the same."

Freddie nodded. "That's right. Don't trust anyone in this sport. *Especially* not your own teammate."

That got laughs from the whole team, including even a chuckle from Stavros.

The day before was the qualifying race, meaning the racers starting positions were determined by their lap times. Nicholas would be starting second on the grid—sandwiched between Serge, who was in first place, and his teammate, Stavros, who was in third place. No one expected the position from him, and Nicholas had already conducted several interviews. He hoped he came across as humble because it wasn't how he felt.

As Nicholas and his father left the team meeting, adrenaline pumped through his system. Every bit of him had felt electric since seeing Miranda. His father hadn't yet asked him about it—to Freddie, winning was everything.

Nicholas and Miranda had been inseparable since he was nine

years old. They had become fast friends after Nicholas started school with her. She had been the only person he had felt able to talk to about certain things he was going through—the death of his adoptive parents, the adoption by his biological parents, and the desire to step into his father's footsteps as a Formula One driver. But that was all in the past.

"Hey, are you ready for your first race? You all warmed up?" one of Nicholas' crew members asked him.

"As I'll ever be." The warm-ups and techniques he had used for a decade had worked well so far; he figured they wouldn't fail him now. In fact, a lot came down to trust. There simply weren't many people in the world that he trusted to care for his career as much as he did. His father was an exception.

"I'm going to get ready," he told his father. "Tell Mom I'm thinking about her and mémé." He failed to mention he was also thinking about Miranda, which he knew his mother and grandmother would be much more interested in than Freddie was.

***

The season's first race took place at the same track where they had done their pre-season testing. Just as Nicholas had hoped, his car outperformed his expectations, just as it had before. The whole race was a blur. It had felt surreal when Nicholas drove past the checkered flag—number *one*.

"Nicholas! You did it. First place! Good race. What a start to the season. This is the beginning of something good," Dylan said over the radio. In the background, Nicholas could hear the whoops and hollers from his team.

He pulled into the first-place stop and kneeled beside his car, overwhelmed and exhausted by emotion. His father was the first to hug him, and he threw himself into the arms of screaming Fairway team members. Nicholas glowed on the podium. He held up his trophy and sprayed champagne with Serge and Stavros, who came in second and third. Nothing could bring him down. But there was something could make it better.

"Congratulations," came a familiar voice after Nicholas was finished with interviews and was on his way to the team meeting to conduct a post-mortem on the race and find out what they did right.

Nicholas turned to see Miranda, the sun streaming through her hair, as she walked towards him with a grin.

"I should say the same for you. Second place isn't too shabby for you guys."

Miranda shrugged. "Neither is first."

Nicholas, feeling emboldened by his win, took a leap of faith. "We're going to be celebrating tonight. You should come."

Miranda smiled, and his heart flip-flopped. He crossed his fingers.

"I shouldn't," she finally said.

Nicholas hid his disappointment well. "No problem. See you around."

As Miranda congratulated him again before taking off, he felt like everything in had led up to this one moment. This one win. His comeback.

That win—he wouldn't it trade for anything. But if there was one thing Nicholas could change, he might have told Miranda how he felt about her. He didn't know if it was the rush or the adrenaline from winning. Maybe it was. But as he watched her walk away, it dawned on him that he could easily see himself saying three words to her. Three words he had felt his whole life. And if he was being honest, he felt like he would feel for his whole life.

EIGHTEEN
Miranda

Now

T he briny, languid air felt like home. March in Monaco wasn't touristy and was one of Miranda's favorite times in the country—*her* country. With her luggage from the weekend at the race dragging behind her down the sidewalk, she hopped into the apartment elevator she now called home. With a two-week gap between races, Miranda had snagged a flight back for some rest and recovery. Serge was in Germany with his girlfriend, who she hadn't yet met, and he was clear about needing some time to clear his head. After the second-place finish to Nicholas' first place, Serge was breathing down her neck about upping their plan.

Miranda didn't believe that Nicholas was doing anything special in a way that she wasn't already training Serge. But drivers had a similar tendency to believe they were the best. Anything less than first place must result from the car, the tires, or, in this case, someone else's unique treatment—certainly not because of their driving. Strangely, even after all her time going to more junior races with Nicholas through their adolescence, he never seemed to think he would win. She thought that perhaps that uncertainty kept him pushing.

Getting into her apartment, she opened the windows and immediately began tidying up. She needed to get her apartment ready and make as much space in the small closet she had as was humanly possible. Her dad had confirmed he was coming before her own flight back to Monaco. She hadn't had any time to prepare. But she was guessing that he hadn't planned the trip with much warning either. She got her spontaneous gene from him. And frankly, she thought that this was going to be very good for him.

***

She was at the airport once again. But she wasn't going anywhere. The arrivals gate was busy. Luckily, she had a taxi waiting nearby. Hopefully, they didn't scoop anyone else before her dad arrived.

"Dad!" she called, waving him over.

He looked his usual self, but with darker bags under his eyes than she remembered. Had they been there before? Somehow, he seemed more fragile as he walked towards her. Was she imagining it?

"*Ma belle*," he cooed as he got closer. "Wow. I can't believe I'm actually here." He looked around like he was on another planet, taking it all in.

She laughed. "I can't believe it either."

The two of them caught up in the taxi on their way to Monaco from the airport in Nice.

"I've missed this view," her father said as he looked out the window, the same way she had when she first arrived. "Gosh, it doesn't feel possible. I've been away from here for so long."

"We always said we'd return," she gently reminded him.

His eyes were glassy, and she knew he was also thinking about Chris. "We did say that," he agreed.

When they arrived at her apartment, Kyle looked around. "So this is home?" he asked.

She laughed a bit awkwardly. "I guess so." *Home* was a tricky concept lately. "You can take the bed," she offered. "I have a cot."

Kyle shook his head. "No. You take the bed."

She rolled her eyes. This could take all afternoon. "We've still got a few hours before dinner. Do you want to explore?"

Kyle nodded, and as they walked out of the apartment, he gripped her hand tightly. "I'm nervous."

She frowned before allowing her face to soften. She took in the etched groove between her dad's brow. Things had been hard for him. He'd lost his partner. This visit wasn't easy for him.

"I know you are. I was too," she said. "I still am, I guess."

He nodded. "At least I have you here."

She linked her arm to his, and they walked toward Monaco. "It will suck," she admitted. "Seeing things that reminded you of him. But—but then it gets easier."

"I hope so," he chuckled.

Miranda thought about how they had always been good at joking together. The serious stuff—not as much. This was going to be the start of something new.

***

Just like the driver she worked with, Miranda could be obsessive—a trait she both loved and found exhausting. If she were going to do her job, she might as well do it to the best of her ability. But she wasn't going to cheat. Walking along the meticulously maintained sidewalk, Miranda followed the directions on her app to trace the course of the Monaco Grand Prix.

Being prepared helped ward off the nervous feelings that tended to flutter up. Miranda wasn't ready for the face she saw ahead of her, coming from a side street.

"Twice in a week. What are the chances?" Nicholas asked, walking towards her. He wore sunglasses and a ball cap, just like he had when she'd first run into him. But going incognito in Monaco wasn't all that important in the off-season. Most of the locals respected people's privacy. Besides, there was always someone *more* famous around the corner.

"I thought you would be training right now," Miranda said. She crossed her arms self-consciously, unsure why she felt the way she did.

"I am."

It dawned on Miranda they were now heading in the same direction.

He motioned towards them. "Mind if I join you?"

Miranda shook her head, but her stomach filled with butterflies. She wasn't sure why. She had felt fine the last time they spoke. The silence they lapsed into felt more natural than awkward.

"Remember that?" Nicholas eventually said, pointing towards the road that led to a small and secluded beach. The two of them had often run off there as adolescents.

Miranda nodded. "It was the last place you and I..."

Nicholas laughed nervously. "Yeah. That fight we had was a big one. Right before you left."

"We weren't really fighters, though, were we? It was just that one."

"Just that one," Nicholas said in agreement.

The two of them lapsed into silence once again. This time, it was more awkward than natural. Miranda bit her lip, wishing she hadn't said anything, but then again, he had been the one to point out the beach.

"What do you think? Do you think it was still the right choice to leave?" Nicholas asked, a teasing tone to his voice.

Miranda felt her cheeks turning bright pink. It brought her right back to that grey evening all those years ago. Even the waves had crashed along the shore with volatility. Nicholas had told her back then that leaving Monaco would be a mistake. And that they should run away together.

She could almost hear his voice in her head from ten years earlier: "What do you think about forgetting it all for a year?" He seemed to have the idea that he could put his driving career on hold for a year and that the two of them could travel the world. It had been the night before she left. Although he was adamant his career could be put on hold, Miranda knew differently. It was an unforgiving sport, and she saw how Nicholas' adoration of her was his weakness. To achieve his dream, he had repeatedly told her that he wanted more in the world; he couldn't have an Achilles tendon.

She had been his weak point.

So, she had done what she needed to allow him to succeed. To achieve his dreams. She'd said a very firm *no*. And the fight had escalated from there. Luckily, everything worked out perfectly for Nicholas. She was happy for him. But another emotion came up, too, one she struggled to place.

Miranda lifted her chin defiantly. "I am happy I left. Look how everything turned out. For both of us."

Nicholas grinned and lightly touched her shoulder. "Thanks. You know, I owe a lot to you for not letting me throw away my career."

Miranda had tried to push those from her mind. "It's no big deal." She would never admit to him how much it meant to her that he was saying the words he was saying.

"Have dinner with me tonight?" Nicholas asked, suddenly stopping. "Please. I'd like to hear about what life has been like over the last few years. And the last dinner we had..."

Miranda knew what he meant. "It was a good icebreaker."

"Exactly. I'd like more than that."

"Like a date?" Miranda faltered.

Nicholas grinned wickedly. "If you want to call it that, I don't see any problems with it. I like a good distraction."

His words were teasing and made her smile, thinking back to their kiss. A lot had changed between them since then. Things had cooled since she started working with his opposition. But with Nicholas smiling, Miranda felt keenly transported back to the same way she had handled all those years ago. A considerable part of her wanted to go.

You work with his rival. You can't date him.

The thought was loud and clear. More importantly, she knew it was accurate. She was in no position to squander her job. Especially now, considering that her dad was here to visit. This was the time to push with her career. She could only imagine the impact it would have on things at the clinic. She relied on word of mouth. So far, her reputation was spotless, and she intended to keep it that way.

She took a deep breath, forcing herself to do the sensible thing. "Thank you," she said politely. "But I'm afraid I have plans with my dad."

"Tomorrow then?"

Miranda shook her head ruefully, burying her head in her hands with a groan. "I'm sorry, Nicholas. I can't risk my job to go on a date with you. My circumstances are...complicated."

Miranda thought Nicholas had never been much good at hiding his emotions. He nodded with a pained look on his face. "I understand. You didn't get to where you are now by taking uncalculated risks."

"And you are—"

"—Definitely an uncalculated risk," Nicholas finished. His confidence seemed to have bounced back. "Well, Miranda, it was great chatting with you. I'll see you around."

"See you at the next race."

"Unless you run into me sooner. Monaco is really more like a small town."

Even though a part of her heart ached at having done what she had just done, she smiled as Nicholas waved goodbye, disappearing behind a corner. Easy come, easy go, Miranda reminded herself. The love of Nicholas' life would always be racing. And she knew that if she wanted what she thought was best for him, it would be best for things to stay that way.

NINETEEN
Nicholas

Now

N
ow that he had been back at his apartment for a full day, there was already a new fleet of yachts in the harbor he didn't recognize. It appeared that a new nightclub had opened up down the street from him, which he had noticed on his taxi ride from the airport.

He had fallen asleep early on his first night home, dreaming that perhaps this new club was where he could convince Miranda to come out. A part of him was still hopeful that she might change her mind and tell him she wanted to grab that dinner after all. What were the chances they had run into one another like that? He didn't know if he believed in fate, but if he did, he would have certainly thought it applied here.

Since Miranda had been there last, he had redecorated. Walking in now, he felt it was impressive, even to his standards. With floor-to-ceiling windows opening onto an iron-wrought balcony overlooking the Mediterranean Sea, it hardly mattered what the rest of the place looked like. But Nicholas had carefully chosen and ordered some modern pieces—some paintings by friends of his that were abstract interpretations of a racecar, a few scattered framed photos of him with his family, an arched leather sofa with two minimalist red chairs across from it, separated by a black marble coffee table. It finally felt like *his* place. He had been ready to share it with someone and make those changes together. A part of him still felt ready.

His phone buzzed, signaling a visitor at the lobby downstairs, and Nicholas picked up. He wasn't expecting company. Maybe it was Miranda?

"Mister Stefano?" came the concierge's voice through his phone. "You have a guest. May I let her up?"

Before asking her name, Nicholas urged the concierge to please let her up. His heart raced as he scanned the surfaces of his home. Through the corner of his eye, he could see his clothes spilling from his luggage. He hadn't bothered putting anything away yet. He threw his clothing into the laundry hamper, put three crumb-covered dishes in the dishwasher, and immediately began to put the items that littered his coffee table into a neat pile. He was done just in time for the knock on the door. He was nearly breaking a sweat when he swung the door open with an ear-to-ear smile. Immediately, it fell.

"Chantal? What are you doing here?"

Her pin-straight hair was smooth and glossy. She wore all black.

"What, aren't you going to invite me in?" she asked, seemingly undeterred by his reaction.

Nicholas, who had been raised to be unfailingly polite, closed his agape mouth and realized that he was inadvertently blocking her from entering his apartment with his arm. Reluctantly, he lowered it.

"Come on in," he managed.

As she often had, Chantal made herself right at home, flinging her presumably new purse onto his dining table and taking a seat on one of the chairs she had once told him she hated.

"You re-decorated," she said, looking around. "I like it."

"Thanks."

"I'll bet you're wondering why I'm here?" she asked in a low voice.

Nicholas took a seat on the new leather sofa across from her. His cheeks were burning. He thought he was over it. Over *her*. But the sting of her betrayal seemed to be hitting him again.

"That's one thing I'm wondering."

"Right. I'll get straight to the point," Chantal said, standing up from the chair and sliding beside him on the sofa.

Nicholas inched over to give them space. He shot up like a firecracker when she inched over with him, choosing to stand instead.

"What do you want?" he asked, unable to keep the frustration from his voice.

Chantal pouted. "I want to talk about what happened. I have news for you. And I don't know who to talk to."

Over his dead body. "You gave up your right to have me as a sounding board when you cheated on me," he said flatly.

"Oh, come on," she persisted. She had never been one to take 'no' for an answer. What she wanted, she usually got. "We were such good friends and could talk about anything before we got together, don't you remember?"

"Not really."

"Well, I do."

He sighed. "A lot was great with us until I found you with Serge. Yeah, right up until then, we were great."

The words hung in the air, and the memories flashed back to him with more pain than he would have guessed. Serge had been his best friend. His only friend in the sport. And when he'd walked in on the two of them...it had taken a long time to recover. He figured he was still recovering.

"Please don't be mad about that. I didn't mean to hurt you. In fact, I have something to tell you about that—"

Nicholas felt his blood nearing a boil. "I think you should leave."

A flash of remorsefulness crossed Chantal's face as she stood up. "Okay. I'm not here to force you to listen."

Nicholas pursed his lips together as she walked towards the door. With no more ammunition to fire off, Chantal left. As the door shut with a thud, he breathed a sigh of relief.

Nicholas walked to his balcony to get fresh air and clear his head. He wished he had some clarity a year earlier when he had met Chantal. He had felt so lost. Desperate to get back into the racing world, unsure of his next steps, and still fuming from how he had been let go from his team years earlier. When he had met her, he was stuck. And she seemed to have been able to smell the success on him before he knew it himself. For all her faults, Chantal had really believed in him. Having her in his corner had been outstanding in a world as competitive and ruthless as Formula One. Or so he had thought.

She had helped him believe he could get to where he was now with the team. The betrayal had hurt more than he allowed himself to acknowledge.

***

Getting out to the water was always a surefire way for Nicholas to clear his head. He walked along the port, where patrons were flitting to restaurants for seaside dinners, and yachters returned after afternoons at sea. It was golden hour, and the sun lazily sank into the horizon. Moments like this reminded Nicholas why he remained in Monaco after all these years.

Moving to a new place would have felt more manageable, especially after his most recent heartbreak. With a new home came a clean slate. He had felt he needed that. But he had gotten his contract with Fairway, and life continued. As it always seemed to. It turned out he did well with distraction. Coming back and especially seeing Chantal brought back some emotions he thought he had long sped by. Monaco was full of the only people he could trust—his family. It also now housed the one person he knew he couldn't trust who had broken his heart.

Trust was paramount for Nicholas. Growing up in a moderately well-known family, intimate details weren't shared with everyone. Only the nearest and dearest heard their funny stories and shared secrets with them. From a young age, his father had hammered it into him: "Be careful who you talk to, Nicholas. Because some people can't wait to pass it along like a bad cold."

He had stopped looking at headlines. They had sent his anxiety into spirals. Curating his image had long ago been part of his plan. Whenever he saw a headline that blasted him, he took it as a personal attack. He knew it wasn't the case but knowing it and feeling it were two different things.

Already, there were rumors through the paddock about Chantal and Serge getting together. He resolutely refused to comment on it. He didn't want to add any fuel to that fire.

He felt a stab of longing as he looked at couples on dates and families together, some taking pictures and others walking hand in hand. After all, he thought he had found his person.

***

The racing season was better than he could have imagined. His performance was unparalleled.

Unfortunately, so was Serge's.

There had been a few more races since the first and the two of them had remained wheel-to-wheel for each race, going back and forth between first and second.

It didn't help that Miranda was clearly thriving in her new role. Serge seemed to have lost all fear on the grid. Nicholas had known about Serge's weaknesses. Now, it seemed as if everything was uncertain.

But he was also doing better than he'd anticipated.

"Keep it up, Nicholas, and you'll be a world champion. We'll have an exciting run next year," his team principal had told him. An unanticipated perk of doing so well was watching Stavros sulk.

After winning another race, he returned to his hotel room, putting him and Serge tied for first in the season. Part of him felt on top of the world.

"Congratulations."

He turned around and saw Chantal walking towards him. She was wearing the hat for Serge's team. *Is she trying to rub it in?*

"Thanks," he said, stopping mid-tracks and taking her in. It wasn't hard to understand why he'd fallen for her. Gorgeous, bubbly, and seemingly down-to-earth. But she also had been in love with someone else. His best friend.

Serge had once been many things to Nicholas. A confidant. A racing buddy. His best friend. It made the competition on the track that much more high stakes. He was surprised he hadn't run into Chantal earlier this season.

"How are you doing?" she asked with genuine concern.

"Fine," he answered quickly. He knew he sounded rude and forced himself to smile. He was glad she had witnessed a race where he beat Serge. That would show him. "How are you?" He cursed himself for asking because, quite frankly, he didn't really want to know.

She shrugged. "I'm good. It's been a busy start to the season."

"I haven't seen you around," he said, immediately regretted it. It sounded like he was looking for her at the races. Which he wasn't. He was scanning Serge's team for another face.

"I haven't wanted to draw too much attention to us," she said.

He bristled at using the term 'us' but tried to hide it.

Nicholas nodded. Chantal wasn't a bad person. He just hadn't been the right person for him. Maybe Serge was that person for her.

"I appreciate that," he finally said. Silence fell between them, and he didn't know what else to say.

"By the way," she began. "If there's anyone who you need to tell about the, uh, situation, I would do it soon. It's going to be hard to hide things soon." She touched her stomach fondly.

He nodded, feeling more emotion than he would ever allow himself to show. He knew he had to tell Miranda.

"Well, I should get going—" he finally said.

"—Wait," she insisted. "Is there anyone special in your life?"

"Why do you ask?" His eyes narrowed. Was she on to him and Miranda?

She sighed. "I just—I guess I've been struggling with feeling guilty."

"Okay," he replied, shifting from foot to foot. Being reminded of what happened between her and Serge hardly made him feel like a winner. And he didn't feel like he had to make her feel better for how things had played out.

"And I wanted to say...I'm sorry." She sighed as if this was a huge accomplishment for her. "I'm sorry. I know I said it before, but I needed to say it to you when emotions were less...heated. I tried when I came by your place—"

He nodded. "—I wasn't ready to hear it."

"Well, thanks for hearing me out," she said softly. "Also, you'll get the signed papers soon. I'm sorry it's taking so long. My lawyers have been trying to get me to ask for more and it's been a battle with them, too, but I've been resolute—I don't want anything from you. The papers should reflect that."

"That's great." He found himself smiling. Things between them felt lighter than they had in a long time. The truth was going to come out soon. For some reason, he didn't dread it the way he had in the near past.

"I guess I would have felt better knowing you were in love too."

"In love?" he asked quickly and regretted it.

She looked sheepish and nodded her head. "Yes. I love him." She put her hand on her stomach, and Nicholas realized what she was talking about.

A part of him softened, although he wondered if he shouldn't have felt upset. "I'm happy for you," he said. And he meant it.

Chantal smiled, this time letting her guard down. "Thank you."

And he could tell she meant it.

"So there's no one special in your life?" she prodded.

He pulled a face. "Not anymore."

"Well, if there is someone you're not going after, I think you deserve it," she said. "You're such a great person."

"I'm focusing on myself right now," he said carefully. "It seems to be panning out. I'm focusing on my career."

"Timing is everything," Chantal said breezily, and Nicholas wondered if she knew something that he didn't.

TWENTY
Miranda

Now

"This morning, I want you to start changing your diet. Not calories, but related to nutrition. We're currently focusing on anti-inflammatories to get your knees in better shape for the race. Sound good?" Miranda instructed. She had met Serge on a beach in Saint-Jean-Cap-Ferrat that morning since he had returned to Monaco the night before. They would do a series of hill runs and strength training before most people had even woken up.

Serge nodded, leafing through the diet plan Miranda had made up for him.

"Now, let's get started. We're currently focusing on neck and upper body since last week we focused more on leg work."

Her nights had been spent researching the muscles in the neck and head, how they responded to the G-forces that drivers were subject to when driving at such high speeds, and particularly the muscle groups that Serge reported the most stiffness. Wherever there was stiffness, Miranda knew that there needed to be strengthening.

She did a series of reflex exercises with Serge, from inexpensive ones, like him catching tennis balls that she dropped, to more tech-driven ones that she had shelled out money for, such as a screen with flashing lights that Serge had to hit each time it lit up somewhere new on the screen. She was happy with his progress, but importantly, so was Serge. Most importantly, so was the team.

"So I heard about your meeting with Griegor," Serge said between heavy breaths as he and Miranda threw a weighted ball to one another.

Miranda threw the ball to Serge's left, which he deftly caught. "And what do you think about it?"

Serge smiled. "I think it is good for you. Good for me, too. It means you have to prove yourself this year. But the only real way to do so is to ensure I win."

Miranda smiled but inside her stomach was in knots. Yes, she had options for her next steps with her career. But sometimes it felt like she was the passenger of her own life. She wanted to be in the drivers seat. Was this what she wanted?

"That's the plan," she said, forcing a smile. "We want you to win. We all do."

Serge held onto the weighted ball. "You're good, you know. Good at what you do."

"I'll be honest though. This might be my last year racing," Serge said.

Now, it was Miranda's turn to hold onto the weighted ball. She nearly dropped it with surprise. "I don't think I heard you," she said, laughing slightly. "The waves are getting to be a bit loud."

Serge smiled kindly. "My girlfriend is pregnant. I don't know..."

Miranda picked up the ball. "Congratulations! That is great news. What is it you're unsure about?"

He shrugged. "I don't know if I'll have the same killer instinct with children. There will be a part of me that worries. If I crash..."

Miranda nodded and threw the ball back to him. She tried to maintain the same even and steady voice as he had. "Maybe kids will give you extra motivation to work harder."

"Perhaps. Or maybe it's a new chapter of my life. Maybe I'm ready for a new challenge, you know?"

Miranda tried to think of a prevailing point to convince him to stay in the game. How would it look if her driver quit at the end of her first year as a sports physician? She disliked what having specific outcomes tied to her success was doing to her thinking.

"Well, you don't have to make any decisions right away," she finally said. "For right now, let's keep an eye on the prize. And that prize is winning the world championship."

He nodded. "You're right about the second bit, keeping an eye on the prize. But there is a bit of time urgency."

"Oh?"

"Chantal wants us to move back to Brazil full-time. The baby is due in January, right after the racing season. So she's putting the pressure on me," he laughed.

Miranda forced herself to laugh, but inside, her stomach was twisting in knots. She had heard Serge's girlfriend mentioned by her first name before. It was the same as Nicky's ex.

***

The car drove as beautifully as Miranda had remembered.

"Don't you love the feeling of wind in your hair?" she asked as they cruised down the street.

"What hair?" Kyle retorted as he patted his head.

It had felt liberating to finally talk about things. It didn't take away the pain, but it took away the pressure building within her.

She could tell it had the same effect on her dad, whose brow had softened since they cried upon seeing that car together.

Now, it was a celebration of Chris' life. At least, that's what they had decided it was.

"Have you seen Nicholas since being here?" her dad asked.

Miranda had evaded the whole Nicholas topic with him so far. Even though her dad had been there for a few days, she had skilfully discussed her work, Monaco, and her dad. Only a little more.

"Yup," she said quickly.

Her dad raised his eyebrows but said nothing. She kept driving.

"And have you thought about whether you want to stay or return to Montreal?" her dad asked.

She was grateful to be driving so she didn't have to see his expression. "I'm just taking it one day at a time right now," she began. "But right now, I'm leaning towards staying."

"Oh yeah?" he replied in an unreadable tone.

"I like it here. I like who I'm becoming. I miss you, though. And Avra, of course."

"She'll have to visit. And as for me..."

"Would you consider moving back?" she asked hopefully.

"I don't know. It's...hard being back here without him."

"I know," she said. It was hard for her dad to be back in Monaco. It was obvious. Memories of Chris and their life together were everywhere. "Thank you for coming," she added.

"And Nicholas? Does he somehow factor into you wanting to stay?"

How did her dad always know? She took a deep breath. "No. This decision is just for me."

TWENTY-ONE

Nicholas

Now

T hree, two, one. Go.

The next race of the season had begun. Nicholas was starting second on the grid after his teammate beat him by a few milliseconds at the qualifying race the day before. Everything in him wanted to win again. It was like a drug. He couldn't get enough once he got a hit of what being first felt like.

On his way to the grid that morning, he signed at least a dozen hats and papers with his signature. He had grinned at everyone who came up to see him.

What a thrill, Nicholas had thought. *I've missed this.*

He figured he shouldn't have been surprised, yet there he was, almost shocked that so many people were in the seats that day cheering him on. He pushed his foot on the gas, doing everything he could to get past Stavros, but it was useless. His cheeks flamed.

Even off the track, it was clear that tension was mounting between him and Stavros, but Nicholas was doing his best to keep a cool head. He wasn't going to do anything stupid. After all, when driving at those speeds, one tiny mistake could be the last.

Behind him was Serge in the yellow Canary. Nicholas relied on his race engineer to help him make his best moves and stay ahead of his competition. He was paying so much attention to what was happening behind him that he wasn't unprepared for what was happening.

"Nicholas, veer left. Do you hear? Veer left."

The voice came over the radio loud and clear as Nicholas narrowly missed Stavros, who appeared to be having problems with his car. Why else would his speed suddenly reduce so quickly?

Suddenly, his teammate's speed seemed to have recovered as Stavros lurched into gear behind him, narrowly missing Nicholas' back wheel.

"He almost hit me," Nicholas said as calmly as he could muster over his radio. "Tell him to back off."

"Copy."

Now, the race order was Nicholas, Stavros, followed by Serge. Still, Nicholas was doing his best to avoid a collision between himself and his teammate.

"What's he doing?" Nicholas muttered as Stavros drove dangerously close behind him.

The nature of the race kicked him into high gear. Through the chicanes and turns, Nicholas braked precisely when the car required and accelerated at most other times. His car purred as it continued to create more of a gap between himself and Stavros.

This was it, Nicholas couldn't help but think. I am going to win. *Again.*

The checkered flag was nearly within sight when Stavros inched ahead at one of the last turns of the race, and the two came wheel to wheel with his teammate, giving him no room to maneuver. Now Nicholas was angry. He was losing precious time with these games Stavros seemed to enjoy. Embroidered in their battle, the two of them watched as Serge soared past them with no one to block him.

With his mouth agape and the feeling of a win having been snatched from him, Nicholas crossed the checkered flag in second place.

When it came to interviews, Nicholas avoided the topic of his teammate. He said he would need to watch the clips to better understand what happened. He congratulated Serge and his team for a second-third finish and said he would work hard to be first next time.

Nicholas was shocked when he sat down with his team to watch the clips. He hadn't been imagining it.

"He tried to hit me," Nicholas stammered.

"Well, maybe it was an accident," his colleague mused, unconvinced. "We will talk with Stavros and see what was on his mind."

"See what was on his mind?" Nicholas balked. "It's plain as day. The footage is right here!"

He left the meeting at the recommendation of Dylan, who said "cooling off" might be the best course of action before speaking directly with Stavros. Nicholas was fuming. His teammate had cost him first place. More importantly, he had risked his life and Nicholas' to undermine him. How low could someone get?

He was so focused on mulling over his anger that he didn't notice Miranda walking towards him.

"Aren't you going to say congratulations?" she asked.

Nicholas looked up to see Miranda grinning cheekily at him. "Sorry, I was just lost in thought..."

"...No, no, I understand," Miranda interjected. "Your teammate tried to run you off the track."

Nicholas' mouth became straight as he shoved his hands in his pockets. He didn't want to badmouth his teammate, but he was dying to review the whole race with Miranda. If only she wasn't working for his opposition.

"Seriously though," she continued. "You're an amazing racer. You would have won without Stavros acting up like that. But you didn't hear it from me." Miranda gave him a wink and came closer, touching his shoulder.

Nicholas offered a feeble smile. Her words of consolation were helpful, and his feelings of rage cooled ever so slightly. "Thanks. And congratulations. Your training is clearly paying off."

Nicholas didn't want to discuss the race further, so he tried to change the topic. "So you excited for the Monaco Grand Prix coming up?"

Miranda smiled. "I'm always excited to be at home."

"Yeah. Traveling is great, but being away all the time is... you know."

Miranda nodded, looking a little weary eyed. "I should get going. We've got our team meeting, and I have more work tonight."

"See you later?" Nicholas asked hopefully.

Miranda smiled back and nodded.

So much for Serge; it turned out that Stavros would be his main problem. But he cheered himself up slightly as he walked back to the team, knowing he had always been a good problem solver.

***

A few weeks had gone by since he last saw Miranda. He had gone on a few dates here and there, but nothing committal. His life was fun. It was exciting. It was chaotic and messy at times.

Most importantly—he wasn't trying to control it.

Six months earlier, Nicholas would have been in the throes of trying to control it all. And frantically panicking when he couldn't.

"So, how are you feeling about the season?" his dad, Freddie, asked him, as they sat in the living room of the Ridgeport's villa.

"It's good. I'm finding that the more I focus on balance, the better I perform."

"What do you mean?" his mom asked.

He shrugged. "I've been paying more attention to what makes me happy outside of racing, too."

"Like what?" Charlotte persisted.

"Tennis, seeing my friends... I'm even thinking about getting a dog."

"Do you think that's a good idea?" Freddie persisted. "Keep your eye on the prize."

164

Nicholas knew his dad meant well. The eye on the prize for him was still winning—however, if he didn't feel good outside of racing, he doubted it would mean much. It was counterintuitive to everything he'd ever thought. And some of him still doubted if this whole idea of 'balance' would pay off.

"He hasn't lost any of his last four races," his mom gushed. "Clearly, he's doing something right."

Nicholas' mémé walked onto the terrace using a tortoiseshell-printed cane. "I invited some friends over this evening," she said. "I figured you wouldn't mind."

He smiled. He adored his mémé and her friends. "Who is coming?"

Her eyes sparkled. "An old friend is in town. Do you remember him? Kyle. And his daughter, Miranda, is coming too.

TWENTY-TWO
Miranda

Now

F or the first time this season, she was starting to think 'winning' meant that all the drivers walked away unscathed. The last race had shaken her to her core. Seeing Nicholas like that, so vulnerable and almost broken, had started to put cracks in the walls she had put up.

And so, putting her best judgment behind her, Miranda knocked on the front door of Freddie and Charlotte's villa, with its bougainvillea spilling off trellises and a sun-faded lime-washed exterior.

Charlotte answered the door, looking straight out of Vogue. Every hair of Charlotte's bluntly cut chestnut mane was in place. However, Miranda had long ago learned that Nicholas' mother wasn't nearly as much of a perfectionist as she had assumed.

"My dear, it's been too long," Charlotte cooed, giving Miranda a warm *bisou* on each cheek.

Miranda felt a welling of emotion as Charlotte gazed at her affectionately. "It certainly has been too long," she said, narrowly avoiding a crack in her voice. "My dad will be here any minute. I'm coming from the clinic today and I think I'm getting here a bit before him."

She had been almost as close with Nicholas' parents as with

him. After all, most of her weekends or weekdays had been spent with the guy since she was nine. Their parents had gotten along famously. But they had lost touch over the years.

"Come on in," Charlotte said. "Nicholas will be here any minute. He just ran out."

Walking through the marble-clad lobby to the living room, Nicholas' mémé, Marguerite, greeted her with a twinkling smile.

"Thank you for the invitation," Miranda said, feeling like she was almost buzzing.

Marguerite looked as pleased as she was. Miranda comfortably sat on one of the two freshly fluffed sofas across from one another. As Freddie made his grand entrance, Charlotte nipped off to the kitchen for sparkling water.

"Oh my goodness, is that you? Little Miranda all grown up?" Freddie said, mockingly squinting as though he couldn't recognize her.

For two people who had gotten a later start to parenting, they liked to make up for it.

"It's nice to see you again, Freddie," Miranda said, hugging Nicholas' dad.

"Tell me you and Nicholas have made up," Freddie said as Charlotte entered with the drinks. "We couldn't stand his last girlfriend."

"*Wife*," Charlotte corrected him.

"What was her name again?" Freddie asked.

Charlotte wrinkled her nose and ignored her husband. "Is he bothering you? Because I can put him outside," she teased.

"It's okay," Miranda assured them. Why had she felt so gleeful upon hearing that Freddie and Charlotte had hated his ex? She stuffed the feeling down as quickly as Nicholas strode into the living room.

"Mom, Dad," he said, kissing his parents on the cheeks. "Sorry it took longer than I anticipated," he said before turning to her. "Hi, Miranda."

There he was. Looking just as he always did—neatly combed hair, a lopsided grin, those molten eyes. Her Nicky. After seeing what happened on the track, she couldn't help but realize how she felt. "Hi," she breathed.

"I just ran out to picked up a bottle of champagne," he said.

She smiled and looked at his parents expectantly. "Are we celebrating something?"

Charlotte looked alarmed. "You, my dear. We are celebrating you."

It was an evening to remember. Kyle had near choked on his champagne, he had laughed so hard. It had been a long time since Miranda had seen him like that and it felt good to see him laugh again. Nicholas had an 'urgent matter' to attend to and suggested Miranda accompany him. His parents and her dad had been insistent she go with him as they had re-filled their glasses.

"Don't be a stranger around here!" Charlotte called as Miranda and Nicholas made their way outside.

"Remember, you're always welcome," Freddie echoed.

Miranda's heart swelled as she thanked them.

"So, what was this urgent matter?" she asked, once the door was closed. The air was cool and it was getting dark.

Nicholas grinned. "I thought it might be fun to let them have their fun and we can have ours."

They walked down the narrow road and onto the sidewalk.

"You almost died in the last race," Miranda heard herself saying.

"Almost. But I didn't," Nicholas replied with a grin. Beneath his lighthearted exterior, Miranda had seen how he felt. Fear. It was beneath the surface, just like an electric current that could only be felt when close enough.

"I don't want you getting hurt this season," Miranda found herself saying.

"That's kind. I would prefer to come out of this season with all my limbs intact."

Miranda took in the sunset as she and Nicholas made their way to the waters edge. Each step they took was at the same pace. And the energy between them had mellowed since she last saw him. He seemed different. Or maybe she did. She wasn't quite sure.

"So, do we dare talk about...racing?" she asked. Things that evening had been going so well. Their parents got along famously. And she was sure that she hadn't imagined the sparks between them.

He took a deep breath. "I suppose so," he said. "It's going to be down to the wire as to who wins."

"Only a few more races this season. It's going to be tense."

"Very."

"How are you doing with that?"

He took a few deep breaths. It was now or never. He figured the news about Chantal would inevitably break any day. And if it changed the way Miranda saw him, so be it.

"I haven't been completely forthcoming about my history with Serge," he said, his voice a little shaky but strong.

"Oh?"

"We used to be friends."

She nodded. "He mentioned that to me."

"That's all he said?" he asked.

Again, she nodded.

Time to rip off the band aid. "You already know that things ended between Chantal and I because she fell for...someone else. That someone else turned out to be Serge. I found them together before she broke the news to me."

Miranda frowned, looking thoughtful as if she was piecing it all together. "Serge's girlfriend is pregnant," she replied, her eyes like saucers.

"Yeah. Apparently they are...in love."

"Wow," she breathed. Turning to him, she reached out to touch his arm. "How come you didn't tell me?"

He shrugged. It seemed silly now that he hadn't. "It's embarrassing," he admitted. "Plus, something about saying it out loud made it feel a little bit too real. I don't know if I was ready to accept the truth."

"And now?"

He felt surer than he had in a long time. "I mean, it sucks. But I think everything happens for a reason. We definitely weren't meant to be. I see that now."

"I'm still processing this," she said lightly. "So I don't really know what to say just yet. But how are you? That's a lot to navigate."

He thought about it. "I feel shockingly okay. *Now*. Not so much then." He let out a laugh as if he could barely believe it himself. "I hope this doesn't affect anything with the work you do. I know you're thriving right now. And I didn't tell you to throw a wrench into things. It's just that you'll either hear it from me or from someone else."

Miranda took her time to answer. "You know, I think it puts some things into perspective for me. I care about my work. But I've stopped putting my sense of success in the outcome. I can't control how other people respond or what they do with the tools I give them."

"Is that a good thing for your work?" he asked, genuinely curious.

"I don't know," she shrugged. "I think so. In some ways, it might make me better at it. Who knows? It's all kind of new."

They fell into a comfortable silence as they walked. Monaco was buzzing. She felt his fingertips brush against hers, giving rise to an electric thrill that ran up her arm.

"I've made a decision about my job. I was going to tell you this before you told me everything about Serge," she told him.

"Oh yeah?"

She took a deep breath, only having concocted the idea the day before. "I don't think I'm going to take either of the job opportunities. I'm thinking about starting my own practice." It felt good to say it aloud. She felt a thrill just saying it. It still didn't feel real.

His eyes widened. "Really? That's... that's amazing. You're going to be incredible."

She laughed, suddenly uncomfortable with the spotlight being on her. "Maybe. It's still just an idea. It's no big deal."

"It is a big deal. Why?

Her cheeks felt hot. "I realized that I was just taking opportunities because they were there. And sure, that's a part of life. But I didn't really feel like I was in the drivers seat anymore."

"Sounds like you're making the right decision."

"Anyways, we'll see." She hoped she didn't sound as nervous as she felt. "I mean, just because I have the opportunity doesn't mean I have to take it. I'll continue working with Serge for the season," she said quickly. "But after that, who knows."

"That's incredible," he breathed. "And...where do you think that will be?"

She smiled. "Monaco. Or at the very least, somewhere nearby."

He grinned. "And how are you feeling about us?" he asked.

"Us?" Her breath caught. She was playing coy, but truthfully she didn't know how to respond.

"I mean, are you still feeling like work is the priority?"

She stopped walking. "Work was never the priority. I needed to be the priority. I needed to put myself and my own needs first for a while before I trusted myself with anyone else's. I needed to give myself some time. Grief, change, figuring out my next steps...It's been a journey to figure that out," she said. "I think work was the excuse."

He looked like he was digesting this. "I see."

She didn't want that to be the end of that conversation. "So to answer your question, at least to answer it as best I can...I feel like there might be room for other things in my life."

He looked hopeful. "Oh?"

She took a step towards him. His cologne smelled warm, mingling with the scent of the sea. His eyes dropped to hers.

"Yeah," she said and leaned in to kiss him. And just like that, she felt all everything she had hoped returning home would bring. With him, she felt at home.

TWENTY-THREE
Nicholas

Now

W *hat was he doing?*

The thought pulsed through Nicholas' mind repeatedly as he pushed his foot full throttle on the gas pedal. Nicholas was the forerunner of the race, and there were only a handful of laps left to go. It usually felt good to be hunted rather than the one doing the hunting. Serge was right behind him, threatening to overtake. Behind Serge was Stavros, who had been charged up like a bull rearing to go since the afternoon.

Looking in his mirror again, Nicholas modulated his breathing. He focused on the give and take the car needed to remain first. It didn't help that his heart leaped in his chest every time he scanned behind him.

Stavros is going to cause an accident, Nicholas thought. Behind him, Stavros was driving dangerously close to Serge, not giving space and even pushing him off the track at times.

Nicholas figured that his best strategy was to stay away from his teammate.

Through sheer determination, Nicholas pulled further ahead, his confidence rising with every millisecond he put between himself and the other drivers. He rechecked his mirrors. It was smooth sailing. He let out a sigh of relief. The race wasn't over yet, but at least there didn't

172

seem to be any immediate threat.

He drove the next few laps without incident. Even his race engineer was quiet. And then it hit him. From out of nowhere, Stavros' car zipped up from behind, clipping Nicholas' left back wheel as his teammate attempted a dangerous pass.

Boom. Crash.

Nicholas' car was spinning. His attention returning to focus, he attempted to grip the steering wheel, but it was useless. The car spun and turned until it hit the side of the wall. He bounced off of that before slowing to a halt.

"Nicholas. Are you okay?" The race engineer's voice was steady, but a hint of panic had crept in.

Nicholas opened his mouth to speak but found himself gasping for air instead.

"Nicholas, I repeat: are you okay?"

"Y-y-yes," he managed.

With shaking hands, Nicholas reached up and lifted himself out of the car. His chest was tight, making it difficult to breathe. His headache was blinding. His ears were ringing. Absorbing what happened around him through a thick fog, a team with a hose put out the flames that had started in his engine. Someone spoke to him and guided him off of the track, but he couldn't pay attention. His eyes were fixed on the checkered flag. And Stavros was driving through it to take first place.

***

The warm rays of the sun shone down on him as he sat with his friends, Marco and Liam, gazing out at the Mediterranean from the boat deck. The last few races had been good to him. A few months had passed since his treacherous first few races and now he was neck-in-neck with Serge for who would win the world champion title. There were only a handful of races left in the season. It was anyone's guess who would take home the title.

Stavros had steadily caused chaos but at least seemed to be causing the most damage to himself—the last few crashes had resulted

173

in damage to his car and his car alone. The penalties he had gotten from his dangerous antics were adding up and with just a few races left in the season, it seemed as though the world championship title was down to him and Serge.

It was almost too good to be true for Nicholas.

"How are you feeling?" Marco asked his friend.

"Never better," Nicholas boasted, leaning back and allowing the autumn heat to relax every muscle in his beat-up body.

"And off the track? How are things with Miranda?" Liam prodded.

Nicholas felt his cheeks turning pink, and it wasn't a sunburn. "It's been good. We're spending time together." He couldn't contain his smile and his buddies clapped him on the shoulder.

"I knew it," Marco said. "You two are meant to be."

"We'll see," Nicholas said, trying to play it off. But he couldn't deny how he felt when he was with her. And how, for the first time in his life, he started to think about a life after racing. And it didn't fill him with terror. In fact, he had imagined a few scenarios with her that had him feeling...almost excited.

***

He clung to steering wheel with all his weight. Serge was ahead of him. His heartbeat pumped through his entire body. His knuckles were white. He pressed the gas pedal with full force, the G-forces pulling on his whole body as he sped through a turn.

If he beat Serge today with enough points, he would win the title.

Stavros had petered out a few races ago, his performance stalling, and today was no different. It fuelled Nicholas to know that it came down to him and Serge. Even though he no longer harboured the same anger and hatred for the other driver as he once had—he wanted to win.

But Serge was leading the race today.

Nicholas focused everything he had on the present moment, forgetting about what was at stake. He wiped his mind of the outcome, channelling all his energy into *now*. With his hands gripping the wheel even tighter, his vision narrowed, and with even and steady breaths, he let go of all expectations and control. There was nothing like the present. It was go time.

World champion! The title was his! Nicholas could hardly believe it. Life was so, so sweet. He drove past the checkered flag with Serge trailing behind him by a few seconds. He passed his opponent in the last lap. No one expected it. It was evident in the roar he could hear from the crowd.

"You did it, Nicholas! World champion!" came the voice over his radio.

"Yes!" he shouted. "Yes!"

The crowd was cheering. He could barely believe it. His heart thudded in his chest, and he did a victory lap around the circuit. This was the moment he had been waiting for!

He parked and jumped out of his car, holding his hands above his head to the crowd's thunderous support. He was a world champion!

A million voices were calling him from a million different directions. Dylan approached him and gave him a giant bear hug.

"I knew you could do it, Nicholas!"

He clapped Dylan on the shoulder. "You believed in me through the journey. Thank you."

Stavros came out and gave Nicholas a hug, although he was unsure if it was for the cameras or genuine. Either way, he appreciated Stavros' words—"No more punching above your weight, no? You rose to the challenge."

"So what do you say," Dylan said quietly. "How's about trying this again for the next few years?"

He was nearly speechless. "Sounds perfect," he said. As Dylan was ushered away, Nicholas ran towards his team—the engineers, mechanics, and everyone who made the races run smoothly. "This win is for you!" he yelled to them all. Their hands clapped his back and kissed his cheeks as he hugged them, feeling like this win meant more than he realized. The hardworking people who went into making the car, his gear, the strategy—it hadn't been just him. As they looked at him, some with tears in their eyes, he felt a huge weight off of him that he hadn't realized he was carrying.

Serge approached him from his car, looking exhausted and slightly defeated. The other driver approached him with a small smile. "Congratulations, Nicholas. You deserve it."

Nicholas smiled. He opened his arms to hug the other driver. Once his enemy. Once his friend. He realized Serge was just a flawed person, like everyone else. And he hoped that Serge was happy.

But was still happy to have beat him.

"You were fierce competition," Nicholas admitted. "And you gave me some good ammunition to beat you." He couldn't help but laugh.

The other driver gave a laugh too and for just a moment, Nicholas wondered if there was a possibility of real forgiveness there. Quickly, he was swept away to more people offering their congratulations.

Out of the corner of his eye, he kept watch for one person out of the corner of his eye.

"Looking for me?"

Miranda's voice cut through the echoing reverberation and as he ran towards her, he wrapped her up in his arms and kissed her. The crowd went wild. No more hiding things. No more worrying about the press.

"Mister world champion," she said, pulling away from him with a grin.

"I don't know what's a better prize. Winning today or you."

"Me, *obviously*," she said coyly. "But world champion isn't bad."

He couldn't contain his elation.

"The reporters are going to go nuts. You ready?" she asked, taking his hand in hers.

He nodded. She was the only person who knew how his anxiety had affected him. He took a deep breath. "I'm ready," he said, knowing it was true.

The reporters were already lined up for him. A team member was walking over and ushering him to a private corner where he could be briefed. For the first time, when it came to the press and his anxiety, he meant what he said.

Because I'm Nicholas Stefano, he thought. *World champion.* He thought it had a good ring to it. And speaking of rings, that wasn't the only kind on his mind.

TWENTY-FOUR
Miranda

Now

T he sky was a pale shade of peach, and the waves gently lapped at the craggy, jagged rocks where the Mediterranean Sea met Monaco. The lobby of the Oceanographic Museum carved into the cliff, was quiet except for a few tourists eager to beat the daily rush and a school group.

"So," she said, looking around. "This is what it's like to officially date a world champion?"

"What do you think?" he asked dryly, the corners of his eyes creased. He hadn't been able to stop smiling all month.

She shrugged. "*Meh*," she said in a teasing tone, before becoming serious again. "I'm kidding."

He walked beside her as they made their way through the museum. The two of them had gone regularly as kids. School trips and moments when they needed to clear their heads. It held a special place in her heart.

"And how does it feel being so...public?" she asked.

The two of them had gone full throttle with their relationship since his last race. They were officially public. And the press hadn't been all kind about it either. Some of the attention of his win had been overshadowed by headlines about him "cheating" on his wife. "Weren't they still married?" she had read countless times. She had run out of steam telling others that they were getting divorced.

No one wanted to hear it. And some people didn't want to consider it. Some people seemed addicted to bad news.

"I'm trying to get more comfortable with the public life," he said quickly. "I don't want anyone else's opinion of me to impact how I see myself."

"That's amazing," she said.

"And you? What are you thinking?"

"About your fame?"

"No," he said, suddenly looking a little pink. "I mean...about us."

She smiled. "I think... I think I'm done with distractions."

He frowned. "Oh."

She persisted. "You're not a distraction. You're my focus. I want us to work."

He felt like he had won the world championship two times over. He reached towards her and kissed her there.

TWENTY-FIVE
Nicholas

Now

H
e sat in his living room, holding the letter from his lawyer in his hands. He breathed a sigh of relief. The papers were finally in front of him. Signed.

"Yes!" he punched the air.

He was officially divorced. As he breathed a sigh of relief, he could truly say that he didn't hold any feelings of resent towards Chantal or Serge.

What a relief. Carrying that around had been exhausting.

Now, this only affected one thing he cared about—which certainly wasn't how he was portrayed in headlines. But he had stopped reading those. He figured he couldn't control how everyone saw him. The only thing he cared about now was that he could go forward with his grand plans.

He looked down at the sparkly ring. It sat in a box in the drawer of his nightstand. It had belonged to his mémé. Soon, it would belong to Miranda.

That is—if she said yes.

"It's gorgeous," breathed his mother as she walked in from the balcony.

"Way to go," said his father, trailing behind her. "What a year you're having."

"The best of my life," he agreed. "This is the one thing that could make it even better."

"Is Kyle on the way?" his mémé asked, fretting with her necklace. It was possible she was more nervous about this than he was.

Nicholas looked at his watch. "Kyle should be landing in a few hours." He turned to his father. "You're still picking him up from the airport?"

Freddie nodded. "Yes. And he texted me before getting on the plane. He's so excited for our families to unite."

"Let's hope she says yes," he said, laughing nervously.

"Of course, she'll say yes!" His mother threw an arm around him.

He grinned as he felt butterflies in his stomach. His adrenaline had been pumping ever since he got the ring. This was more nerve-wracking than going wheel-to-wheel in a race. This was possibly the best decision he'd ever made. And that included climbing in a race car for the very first time. For the first time, someone mattered to him more than the sport. And if that wasn't enough, he didn't know what was.

He couldn't wait to see the look on Miranda's face. Avra would be travelling alongside Kyle; but Miranda didn't know it yet. He couldn't wait to meet Miranda's best friend. In fact, Miranda had mentioned that she thought Avra and Markus might be a match made in heaven, if only they had the opportunity to meet. He had never played cupid before, but perhaps this trip would have a few unexpected twists in the road for Miranda's best friend. He had reached out to Avra online, letting her know that he was planning to propose and celebrate with family (and Miranda considered her family) and had proceeded to book the flight for her. Miranda was going to flip.

His parents were joining him for lunch at his place before the sunset drive he had planned with Miranda. After, their families and friends would join them to celebrate.

Again—if she said yes.

"Knock, knock!" his mémé walked in without actually knocking, letting herself in with confidence. "I am here!"

He walked over to greet his grandmother with a kiss on the cheek.

"You haven't proposed to her yet, have you Nicholas?" his mémé asked as she took a seat.

"Tonight."

"Good," she said. "And make sure the wedding is soon. I don't have much time left."

"Mémé? What's wrong?" he asked, suddenly worried. Did she have a health scare? She was older but in great health. He struggled to imagine life without her.

"Nothing," she brushed him off. "I have a new beau in Italy. I plan to spend much of next year travelling with him. So a wedding sooner rather than later would be ideal."

His eyes widened. "A new man?"

His mémé chuckled, her eyes sparkling. "You're not the only one with love in your life."

Nicholas smiled and told his grandmother she'd have to fill him in on the details. As his family chatted amongst themselves, already planning the wedding, he couldn't help but smile. Everything he had worried about a year earlier had resolved itself. The panic attacks and anxiety had been subsiding. And he'd even won the world championship title. He didn't think life could get any better. But he thought about how none of it meant what he hoped it did without Miranda.

It had always been about Miranda. From when he was a kid. Trying to impress her was what got him racing in the first place. Her leaving fuelled the fire she'd left in her absence. Now that she was back, everything in his life had seemed to fall into place. Finally, finally, finally—he felt like the timing was right.

TWENTY-SIX

Miranda

Now

T he car chugged up the hill. Traffic was piling up behind them and the melodic music that Nicholas had put on at the beginning of the drive was being drowned out with the sound of car horns. The sun was beating down with the top down on the convertible and a bead of perspirations trickled down her forehead.

"It was working perfectly this morning," Nicholas sputtered, his hands gripping the steering wheel as he looked into the rear-view mirror, visibly flustered.

"It's just our luck with this car," she teased. "I don't think I can remember a single time it worked perfectly with the two of us. It always slows down."

"No. No, no, no, no, no," he said, his eyes widening. "It's not that. Maybe the car gives us a chance to slow down. And focus on the moment, rather than speeding off to the next thing. The journey, and whatnot."

The car persisted up the hill before Nicholas pulled over and slowed to a stop. A parade of cars sped past them. Theirs made a few gurgling noises before turning off completely.

She turned to him expectantly. He looked back, eyes like saucers.

183

"I think we're out of gas," he said in disbelief.

"Out of gas?" she echoed.

He shook his head. "I can't believe it," he muttered beneath his breath. "This has never happened. My mind was elsewhere. I just wasn't focused on the gas tank indicator..." he trailed off.

Miranda began to laugh. "Something about this car just brings us bad luck."

"No!" he said with enthusiasm. "This car brings good luck. Remember the last time this happened to us?"

She remembered how they had gotten stuck on that journey to Menton all those years ago. "We did eventually get going again," she admitted.

"And it's where we had our first kiss," Nicholas continued.

"And second kiss," she added, her mind flitting to the garage.

"Miranda, I love being stuck on the side of the road with you. I love being with you. Being with you makes me love the journey. My whole life, it has always been about the destination. My happiness has always been tied to achieving something. Or being 'someone'. But when I'm with you, nothing else matters."

She felt herself blushing and she knew it wasn't the heat. "Oh my. I wasn't expecting that."

He continued, reaching out to hold her hand. "You're kind. You go after your dreams. And I don't think you think of yourself this way, but you're fearless. It takes guts to move all around the world, taking leaps of faith that it will all work out, and starting your life again. Being with you makes me want to slow down time. It's never a race to the finish line with you."

Miranda's heart felt like it could explode. She squeezed his hand. "Nicky, that's the sweetest thing I've ever heard. I feel the same way about you. I love you. I always have. Always will."

She would never forget the look on Nicholas' face. Studying him, with his beautiful long lashes and open expression, she felt a way she had never felt before.

After a moment, got stepped out of the drivers seat and made his way to the passenger's door, which he opened and dropped to one knee.

"Miranda Thatcher—I wanted to do this at a cliff at sunset. But if I'm the happiest man in the world being stuck on the side of a road with you, in this old car we used to drive around in as I fell in love with you way back then; well, I can't think of anything more fitting. I love you, Miranda. I love our journey and destination. I want to spend the rest of my life with you, and I hope you feel the same way."

Time slowed down. Nicholas reached into his pocket and pulled out a ring box. Her breath caught as he opened it, revealing a sparkling diamond.

"Will you..."

"Yes!"

She leaped into his arms with abandon. Her heart swelled, and she felt joy radiating from her fingertips to her toes.

"Yes," she said once again, kissing him and allowing him to slip the ring onto her finger. It fit perfectly.

"Yes?" he asked, his whole face illuminated with joy.

"Yes," she said softly. "Yes, yes. A million times yes."

TWENTY-SEVEN
Miranda

Ten years ago

"I can't believe you're really going," Nicholas told her.

"I can't believe it either."

Their toes sat beneath the waves, dipping in the Mediterranean as summer's last bits faded. Was she making the right decision? He seemed to echo her sentiment. She was leaving tomorrow.

"Tell me why again you guys are going?" he asked.

"Sometimes you need a change," she said, repeating the words she had with her dads the night before. "We're going to have an adventure. See the world. If it's meant to be, we'll return. What's meant to be...and all that." She trailed off, feeling slightly less sure of her words than before.

Nicholas looking at her with those gorgeous eyes of his didn't help. Neither did the kiss they had shared. He leaned in.

"Don't!" she cried.

He recoiled, visibly hurt.

"I didn't mean that to come out so...intensely," she said. "It's just...I think it's going to be harder. The more we draw this out."

He nodded, sadness and understanding in his expression. "Okay then."

She pulled her toes from the water and sat cross-legged, picking up a smooth stone and running her fingers over its smooth surface. "Who knows? Maybe you and I will have the chance to... I don't know..."

He looked hopeful and sad at once. "Maybe. A lot is going to change in the next year."

She nodded, fixing her gaze at the horizon. It was too hard to look at him.

He continued. "Like you said, though. If it's meant to be, maybe you'll come back."

"Or you'll come to Canada," she added.

"Who knows," he said as a statement than as a question.

"I'll miss you, Nicky."

"I'll miss you too."

"Who knows," she echoed him.

"Who knows."

TWENTY-EIGHT
Nicholas

Now

H e looked around the sparsely decorated office. The small lobby led to an office in the back. The lobby had a few grey chairs and a worn carpet, offset by large fluorescent lights on the ceiling.

"This looks—"

"—I know," Miranda jumped in. "It's not quite the way I want it yet..."

He took a step towards her and wrapped his arms around her from behind. "I was going to say it looks perfect."

They were standing in Miranda's new office. It was about twenty minutes from Monaco—as long as there was no traffic. She had registered with the French Medical Council and as soon as she had, she'd found the listing online and booked a showing immediately. She signed it right after seeing it.

"You really think so?" she asked him, looking around. "I'm having doubts."

He smiled. "It's going to be great. Remember, it doesn't have to be perfect right away."

She nodded. "I can't wait to start building my practice and getting back to the thing that I love most—helping people be healthy through sports. It's why I got into this niche in the first place. I'm going to see lots of sports injuries, I'm sure, but focus most of what I do on everyday people who have regular injuries, and help them get back to living healthy lives."

"I think that sounds incredible."

She beamed. "I think my dad would be really proud."

"I think he would be, too. Kyle is, too."

Miranda nodded. "Yeah. He's going to come visit in a few months and try making it out here more. I'm going to head back to Montreal to visit before spring."

"So is this what you had expected when you came out here?" Nicholas asked her, taking a seat on one of the grey chairs. "Paging Doctor Thatcher. I am self-diagnosing myself as having too much love. Can you help me?"

She laughed, taking a seat beside the small reception desk. "Not a chance. I'll have to refer out."

They lapsed into silence, looking around. "But in all seriousness," she began. "This isn't at all what I expected. But I'm glad. It seems like everything just worked out."

Nicholas matched her smile. "I think that had more to do with you than fate."

She shrugged. "Perhaps. But I'm still glad."

The two of them unpacked the office and put up her degrees. Every so often, Nicholas observed as Miranda would look around, as if in awe of the life she was building for herself.

Silently, he felt in awe as well. If someone had told him a year earlier that he would be where he was, he never would have believed it. It felt like life was too good to be true. But it wasn't. His anxiety still reared up from time to time but it was getting better. Sometimes, acknowledging how good things were made him worry that something bad would happen. He reminded himself that eventually, a new challenge would pop up. But he couldn't anticipate every curve life threw at him. He took it all in, acknowledging how far he had come, too. Life wasn't a race. And he felt confident with his ability to navigate whatever roads were ahead, especially with Miranda alongside.

EPILOGUE
Nicholas

Now

" How are you enjoying wedding planning?" Nicholas' mémé asked the two of them.

"We're loving it," Miranda said, looking at him as he nodded. "We're thinking something simple."

His mémé nodded. "And your practice? How is that?"

Miranda grinned. "I have more clients than I anticipated," she said. "It's going well."

"They're flocking to her," he boasted. "She's helping so many people live their happiest, healthiest lives."

Miranda brushed him off, but it was true.

"And you, Nicholas? How are you doing?"

He thought about it for a moment. "Since signing for a few more seasons, I'm a bit nervous. I mean, I won a world championship with them. Some people are calling me nuts."

"What do you think?"

"I'm learning to tune out other people's unkind words," he said. He'd been working with a therapist Miranda had recommended. It was helping. "Although I think that there's some truth to their concern. I'll have to wait and see."

"Lots of change," his mémé remarked.

"I'm not as scared of change as I used to be," he admitted.

His mémé and Miranda exchanged a smile.

"Champagne?" his mémé asked, popping the bottle and pouring a generous helping into her glass.

Miranda looked up and said nothing. As the trio toasted, she brought the glass to her lips but didn't sip.

He'd never known her to turn down champagne.

"Are you feeling all right?" he asked her quickly.

Miranda looked up, her eyes suddenly glassy. "Uh, Nicky, I'm glad you feel better about change. There's something I need to tell you..."

The End

About the Author

KAYA QUINSEY HOLT is the author of A MONACO MINUTE as well as several romance and women's fiction books. Her books have sold worldwide, have been translated into multiple languages, and adapted for audiobooks. She lives in Canada with her husband and son.

www.kayaquinsey.com

g @KayaQuinseyHolt

🐦 @KayaQuinseyHolt

📷 @KayaQuinseyHolt

BB @KayaQuinseyHolt

—

Other Books by Kaya Quinsey Holt

Maybe in Monaco

The Marseille Millionaire

The Belles of Positano

Fate at the Wisteria Estate

A Date at the Wisteria Estate

Paris Mends Broken Hearts

A Coastal Christmas

Valentine in Venice

Printed in Great Britain
by Amazon

40872316R00119